HOLLIN'S
HEIR

Book One of the
Sentinel Dawn Series

L. G. Ransom

Washington, DC, USA

HOLLIN'S HEIR

© 2013 By L.G. Ransom
All rights reserved.

ISBN-13:978-1481019316
ISBN-10:1481019317
Printed in the United States of America.

Cover Art:
Journey Into Midnight © 2011 © 2013 L.G. Ransom
All rights reserved.

Previously published as: Sentinel Dawn, Journey Into Midnight

DEDICATION:

For my children, who wanted to hear more stories about magical robots and intergalactic adventures.

May the power to dream live forever.

PROLOGUE

Irage walked through the dimensional gateway to his garden home in Annon, closing the portal on the mortal plane with a heavy heart. For the first time in nearly ten thousand years, he mourned deeply and inconsolably. Blindly his weary steps took him to the edge of a white cliff overlooking a wide, brightly sparkling lake. There he sat, leather and metal-clad legs dangling over the chalk-like edge, dark brown eyes staring mindlessly out over the beauty of the panorama before him. It was the end of another era.

It didn't take long for his wife, Leary, to join him. Within seconds of his arrival, she had detected his mood and understood his breaking heart. Wordlessly she lowered herself to sit beside him, long and beautiful arms reaching out to encircle him. He didn't resist, but simply allowed himself to be drawn into her embrace and comforted, like a little child, his head coming to rest against her tiny chest. They remained like that for a long time, then he broke the contact and sat back up.

"Hollin is dead," he said simply.

"I know," she returned, her voice full of loving support and compassion for his loss. "You really must try not to become so attached," she counseled gently. "Humans have such short lives."

Irage didn't respond. He couldn't answer her just yet. Leary hadn't been born to the human world as he had. She was only connected to it through him. Even now she could empathize, feel his grief, and understand his pain, but she would never experience it for herself.

It was his choice to remain with her in Annon. He had elected to join in their fight against the evil Uhnman. He had chosen to become an "immortal" like them, to help them understand and navigate the temporal universe he came from, but his soul remained firmly linked to his home dimension. He craved human attachment, needed the company of those who understood the plethora of ever-varying emotions that simply confused the immortals. But attachment came at a price. Humans were mortal. He was not.

"Has Hollin's Sentinel decided upon a new companion, or will it need assistance choosing?" she asked with great care and consideration for his grief, her voice gentle and sweet, but the question was typically Annonian, and it irritated him.

Always back to business, he thought bitterly. *With no regard for a life that is no more.*

"Darling," she crooned in response, hearing his thoughts as easily as if they'd been spoken out loud. "I don't mean to inflict more pain, but I must know. Without a human partner, the Sentinels must assume a latent state. They are vulnerable. The Uhnman have been strengthening their forces. The evil ones know that our side is weakened, that most of the remaining guard are sleeping, waiting for the next generation to activate them. With Hollin gone, they will take advantage of Phoenix's dormancy."

"Phoenix is not dormant. Hollin transferred it to another

PROLOGUE

partner himself," Irage answered bitterly. "Both agreed it was for the best, but it's what hastened his death. He sacrificed the last years of his mortal life ensuring the Sentinels would be ready for the next battle."

"Such valor," Leary whispered, impressed and understanding better than the others of her kind how precious humans regarded their own short lives. "Such insight."

Irage turned and regarded his wife blandly. She took a human form to please him, to make him more comfortable in a realm that contrasted greatly with the one he'd originated from. Her shape was nearly perfect: elegant, soft, and very pleasing. Only her eyes belied her true origin. They sparkled and glowed with otherworldly colors. He loved her with all his heart, but there were times when the differences between them were difficult to overcome.

"Phoenix chose the girl you had reserved to companion Eale," he replied, almost bitterly, pleased with the widening of her ethereal eyes and the little O of surprise that formed on her lips.

"Well then," she responded, stunned and sitting back a little to collect her racing thoughts, "this is a development."

"A development?" he asked, his anger rising.

"She's one of mine," Leary answered plainly, too focused on her own racing thoughts to notice his mood had shifted from grief to irritation. "I will have to accelerate things, bring the boy to her earlier, and make sure they're securely bonded and attached emotionally. She'll need his stability and strength. It's not likely she'll be able to transition to pairing with Sentinel on her own; I haven't prepped her for it. Poor little thing; she's still a child. I don't know what the lot of you were thinking. She can't possibly be mature enough to handle the evolution taking place; she'll need a great deal of guidance and help."

"She's mine," Irage growled. "Hollin left her to me. He personally asked me for my sworn oath to guide her. I will not ignore a death wish."

"Irage, my love," Leary crooned, "I feel the grief you suffer for your friend as surely as if it were my own, but we must detach emotion from the task at hand. The Unman are rising; we must meet their challenge. I have followed the girl since her birth, planned, and—"

"No," he interrupted firmly, eyes hard. "Phoenix has always been under my command. It's strong-willed, temperamental, prone to making its own choices and ignoring orders, yet it has always listened to me. You have the boy; you will find a new candidate for Eale."

"Irage, please be reasonable," Leary countered gently, laying an elegant hand softly on his arm.

"Promise me, Ilearia," he countered, using her full name to add weight to the demand and emphasize his seriousness. "Give me your solemn oath that you will leave her to my guidance and not interfere."

"Very well," she sighed in resignation, giving up on the matter far too easily to grant him any confidence she was taking the matter seriously. "Come walk with me through the gardens," she added, changing the subject abruptly. She rose and extended her hand in his direction. "It will take your mind off the grief in your heart."

PROLOGUE

1

CHAPTER ONE

Years later, Kricket would recall that first morning to historians with a wistful smile and simply shrug. There was nothing remarkable about it. It was just your average midweek morning, and she had a fairly average problem. It had been almost a year since the invaders had arrived and her world had come crashing down around her, so an average day with an average problem was actually pretty nice. The sun was shining, the birds were singing, and there was a skip to her step, one that had been missing for a long time, which had suddenly found its way back in her stride.

"William!" she called, smiling and waving as the object of her search came into view. She'd found him exactly where she thought he'd be: alone with his computer.

He looked up from his small laptop and graced her with a pleased, if slightly uncomfortable, smile. It wasn't every day someone actually sought him out, but, then again, this particular person had known him his entire life, just over eighteen years, and had continued to befriend him long after many childhood acquaintances had realized his oddness and melted away. That was fine with him. People, in general, made him nervous.

"Mom's not happy with me," she said with an exaggerated

CHAPTER ONE

sigh, flopping down beside him on the back steps of the building. She was totally at ease with him despite his unusual choice of mismatched clothing and thick shock of wild and unruly blond hair.

"So she informed me this morning," he answered, absently pushing the dark lenses of his sunglasses back up the bridge of his nose. "I'm supposed to talk some sense into you…if that's even possible," he added.

"Help?" she asked in a mewling tone. For good measure, she added a comically pleading pose, which generally made him laugh, complete with pouting lip, wide eyes, and folded hands.

Despite his best efforts, he genuinely smiled, then pressed his lips together to hide it.

"She's forbidden me from going out after dark," Kricket continued. "That's going to ruin everything. She'll listen to you. Talk to her. Help me convince her she's wrong."

"Anyone who disagrees with you is wrong," he replied gruffly, turning his attention back to the screen in dismissal.

"Not always," she countered defensively, "just most of the time." She added a cocky smile and a knowing twinkle in her eyes. It was an old argument between them and not one that she took seriously. She and William had grown up together, and he was more a brother to her than her own siblings had been.

"Try seeing things from her point of view," he advised gruffly, raising his head up to contemplate the spring day around him, then turning his attention back to his computer. "You're all she has left."

Unhappy with his reply, she responded with a disgruntled sound and turned away, gray eyes searching the busy quad around them. The mottled ground and half burnt trees, victims of the last round of enemy fire, didn't in any way resemble the imaginary garden that she retreated to in her dreams each night. Dreams of the garden had kept her sane since her grandfather had died. It was her personal fantasy world: the only safe place left to retreat to as the war raged around her and hunger punished her young stomach.

"They're looking for resistance volunteers," she said cautiously, gauging his reaction. When he ignored her, she growled in frustration, kicking her heel against the concrete steps. "Come with me," she urged.

"And do what?" he asked in a distracted manner. The only reason he was even still there was his own guilt. When the invaders had first arrived, he and Kricket had sworn a pact to always look out after one another, but he was leaving soon, and he couldn't even tell her why.

Kricket and her mother weren't being evacuated with the other colonists. Her mother had refused to consider the idea. They would both stay behind and take their chances with the rest of the general population. The thought made his stomach sink, but there was nothing he could do about it; the choice was her mother's, not his.

"You can help," she countered in a serious tone. "I don't know anyone who's better with computers and electronics. You could be a huge asset. We could go together to the—"

"The government has better computer people than me," he mumbled, eyes still consumed with whatever data was pouring across his screen. "As well as trained soldiers to fight."

"The government is still denying there's a war," she spat back. "They're still insisting that it's miscellaneous terror attacks. You've seen those things. I don't see how anyone can claim they're from this world; no one can. Meanwhile people are disappearing left and right. The infrastructure's collapsing, there's no food, no water…"

"Your friends don't want me, Kricket. I make them nervous," he replied simply, eyes still on the screen even though he'd stopped reading it. "Besides, your mom's already lost four children," he added solemnly, reminding her of how her brothers had died. Privately he couldn't disagree with her. The local military didn't have a chance against what they were facing. Forming local resistance groups, however, was suicide. He began to say so, but as soon as he opened his mouth, all sound but that of the warning sirens was drowned out.

CHAPTER ONE

Without thinking, she automatically grabbed his arm tightly in alarm. She was no coward, but all of them had learned to dread the sirens. It meant the invaders were back. It meant that something, or someone, was going to be blown to pieces, like her brothers had. You never knew when; you never knew who. It was just the terrifying reality that life had become.

"Oh my god. They're back!" she shouted, urgently pulling at him to stand up.

"Get to the shelter!" he yelled back, slamming his computer closed and jumping up. Almost without thinking, his fingers found the small panic button that would alert the crew of the *Nadir* that the Roan were attacking the colony again. She didn't move though, just stared in wide-eyed horror across the courtyard. Following her gaze, he saw them. There were at least a dozen gray-skinned, armored soldiers steadily marching toward them, flanked by two spider-like, armored attack vehicles.

***

"That's a little overkill, don't you think?" the tech asked as the monitor in the ship's command center revealed Malizore's drones making their appearance on the planet's surface. "No less than two battlepeds and half a squadron. The boy's barely considered technological staff, not even a fighter. His file says he's doing diplomatic work with the colonists."

"He's Professor DeSirpi's son and a main contact for the evacuation; transport him out of there," Ceya ordered from her command station behind him, her eyes watching as the monitors unveiled the scene on the planet's surface below. Malizore was up to something more than going after the Federation's top scientist's offspring; she just wasn't sure what. She wasn't even exactly sure why a battleship like the *Nadir* had been pulled from the front instead of a smaller ship.

"I can't. The girl," he responded, fingers flying over his console. There were strict rules that governed the exposure of their technology to the indigenous population, and he couldn't circumvent them without a direct order from his superiors. "She didn't run to the shelter with the others," he explained.

"If Malizore has figured out who the boy is, he can't go back anyway. Transport him out of there," she ordered calmly, rising and coming to stand behind him.

"No good," he responded, rapidly switching from one control command to another in an attempt to find a way to carry out her orders. "The signal won't lock. They're jamming us."

***

"Into the building!" William yelled over the sound of the sirens, strategically placing himself between his friend and the danger quickly approaching them.

They turned and ran the six steps, two at a time, separating them from the back doors. The thick, protective doors, however, had locked at the first sound of alarm. No amount of pounding on them would entice anyone on the inside to open them. The people on the quad below screamed and scattered, heading for the front of the building, which would be the only access to the inside until the attack had finished, and William cursed that he hadn't remembered that rule sooner.

"Follow me," he urged, then grabbed her hand for good measure, pulling her behind him.

There was no going back down the steps. The enemy had zeroed in on them and was fast approaching, so he moved to the side rail, swinging his legs over the protective metal bars and encouraging her to do so as well.

"Jump!" he commanded without giving her time to think about it. Hand still secured around her wrist, he pulled her over a row of high hedges and to the gravel below. They hit the ground with a thud, and she fell forward, skinning the palm of her hand and smacking her knee. Fortunately she was able to spring back up quickly, so he shot forward, pulling her firmly behind him. She didn't argue; no one captured by the invaders ever came

CHAPTER ONE

back. They made remarkably good progress, considering they were on foot, but they were no match for soldiers on mechanized transports.

They were surrounded within seconds, and William stopped short, heaving for breath. He did his best to keep her behind him, but she had spun around and flattened her back against his, apparently trying to protect him as much as he was trying to protect her. The thought amused him. She was tiny for a girl, barely over five feet tall, with the top of her head hardly rising to his chest, but it was also a bit endearing. He doubted anyone else would have tried. In fact, he'd probably be the first one offered up if the invaders demanded a sacrifice in return for the safety of the building.

"Stay behind me," he ordered in a rough voice, trying hard to step up to the situation and be the man his father assured him that he could never be.

The tone surprised her, and it showed on her face. He was usually soft spoken, not authoritative at all. She had known him all her life, but there was nothing familiar about the young man whose back was pressed against hers. He seemed taller, stronger. The thought would have been more disturbing if they hadn't been surrounded by alien soldiers and about to die.

"Kinda hard to stay behind you when they're circling around us," she fired back. Despite the pounding of her heart and the adrenaline pumping through her veins, she wasn't nearly as scared as she thought she'd be. Then again, she had no intention of being taken alive; so perhaps that helped. There was a lot less to worry about if you were prepared to die rather than be captured.

They had begun a type of shuffling dance. Round and round, the soldiers circled them. Watching, waiting, staying ready, and searching for any opening either could find. Then William abruptly stopped. "*Malizore*," he breathed. The fear in his voice not lost on her.

She had no idea who he was talking about, but the strange-looking warriors had suddenly snapped to attention. Like a little mouse who was afraid to leave its burrow, she cautiously peeked around his arm but honestly wished she hadn't.

The person he'd called Malizore was massive. Well over six feet of muscle and armor, he appeared to be human, but he was also terrifyingly disfigured. This skin on the left side of his face looked as if it had been melted off. The ear was gone, and a thick, intricately carved piece of silver metal was bolted into his skull, covering the eye socket. The exposed skin of his arms was thickly tattooed and lined with angry scars. He walked confidently toward them, as if he considered them of no importance.

"Where's your father, boy?" he growled in a deep baritone. "Tell me, and you just might live to see him again."

William remained silent, but Kricket could feel him shiver, or perhaps that was just her shivering; she wasn't sure. She ducked back behind him, but that proved the wrong thing to do. Malizore hadn't noticed her at first, but he'd seen the movement. An instant later, two gray soldiers grabbed her arms and dragged her forward.

"Leave her alone!" William shouted, and more of the guard lunged forward to restrain him as well. He struggled valiantly, kicking and thrashing.

Malizore threatened, "I will kill her instantly if you fight."

William immediately did as he was told. In response, the large man smiled evilly, pleased to uncover the boy's weakness so quickly. "My, my," he crooned in a rumbling purr, strutting forward until he was only a few inches from her. "What a pretty little bird the nets have captured."

At his silent command, the soldiers released her, and she stood facing him for the first time, eyes wide and body paralyzed with fear. He placed a thickly calloused finger under her chin, lifting it so that she was forced to look at him. "*Very pretty*," he confirmed as her large gray eyes met his one remaining black one. "I shall have a great deal of fun with you, little one. Tell me, son of Piero, how long do you think your little friend here will last in my bedchamber?"

CHAPTER ONE

In response William lunged forward again in outrage, surprising Kricket with his bravery, but Malizore had already anticipated the move. In one swift, sudden movement, his massive hand was around her throat. She managed only a small, surprised little gasp before all airflow in or out ceased completely.

"Tell me where your father is," he growled, his one eye leaving the girl and fixing dangerously on the boy. "We had an agreement; now he's disappeared. Where did he go?"

For the first few seconds, Kricket tried vainly to pry the iron-like fingers from her neck, but it was no use. It seemed an odd way to die, not entirely unpleasant once the initial pain was numbed by the giddiness of lack of oxygen. But she hadn't survived the initial attack a year ago, and every hardship since, merely to be suffocated by an overgrown pig.

She regarded him as cautiously as a cornered animal, relieved his attention had left her to focus on William. He obviously hadn't thought she'd put up any resistance, and, in fact, there was shockingly little she could do. He had, however, left her hands free to claw uselessly at his fingers, and that would prove to be a serious mistake on his part.

Malizore wasn't much concerned with her. She was young and small and hadn't put up much resistance. His grip was fixed easily around her throat, so he saw no need to hold her out and away from him. In fact, it felt rather good to feel her collapse against him as the life drained out of her. Realizing she had very little to lose, she allowed her hands to drop, carefully positioning her right hand close to a small knife holder behind her back. She'd begun carrying it after the first attacks—more for safety against other humans than any alien she might encounter. Life had been difficult, and she'd found herself cornered by more than one scary male in the shelters. She braved a slight glance at her assailant, but a hazy fuzz had surrounded everything, making it difficult to focus. He seemed preoccupied, his head turned, and that was good enough for her. Figuring it was then or never, her fingers grabbed the hilt hidden under her shirt and pulled it out.

The first stab simply bounced off, and she felt a moment of true panic, realizing that she would probably die at his hands without being able to do anything about it. The second stab was driven by a pure, primal desperation to survive. Fortunately she got lucky. Her arm flew backward and then, with all her waning strength, she swung inward instead of up, finding the one section of his armor that was ever so slightly flawed.

If she hadn't been so small, if he hadn't been so lax, if she had stabbed straight on instead of from the side, it would never have worked. As it was, her hand hadn't come up and out nearly as far as she thought it had. Instead, it simply rebounded off his armor, then descended almost sideways through the slip of material that lined the joint between his leg armor and his codpiece—directly into his groin. In response, Malizore froze midsentence; his one eye widened, and the vise grip on her neck automatically released.

The next few seconds seemed to play out in extreme slow motion for everyone involved. William simply stood in stunned amazement as Kricket tumbled silently to the ground. Then, looking up, he spied the small knife handle and realized what she had done. Before he could react though, a rescue team arrived in response to his emergency alarm, and Malizore's warriors had surrounded their leader protectively and transported him safely away from the scene.

Flashes of color seemed to surround Kricket. She couldn't hear anything except the pounding of her heart and was surprised to feel nothing as she hit the ground. A bright green helmet seemed to lean over her momentarily, but she wasn't entirely sure it wasn't the just the sunlight and the long spring grass playing tricks on her. She wondered absently if she was dead, then everything slowly faded into a blissful darkness.

CHAPTER TWO

Unaware of the events on the surface of the planet below, Coltame had fallen into a much deeper sleep than he had expected. Engrossed in his dream, he moved silently, but with considerable anticipation, down a familiar wooded path, then paused at the fog-laced entrance to his family's ancestral garden. It had been more than six years since he'd been called to this realm, and he'd long ago assumed his ability to travel there had left him.

He didn't have to wonder if he would find the spirit just beyond the ancient entryway; she had always been there. From his earliest trainings in the Sight, he found his way to the same ghostly facsimile of his family's long gone ancestral estate and to the same apparition; it was his only success with the innate talent the scribes assured him that he had.

She didn't disappoint him. Almost before the old metal gate had whispered closed behind him, he heard the childlike ripple of delighted laughter. Whether she was a goddess or a nymph, he didn't know, but she was always there. He quickened his pace down the path, then stopped abruptly as he rounded the corner. There was no child waiting for him this time but a grown woman. It startled him. He was so used to the pixie that anything else was slightly disturbing.

"I warned you," she reprimanded without preamble, standing and turning to face him proudly. She was still remarkably small, he realized. She rose no higher than his shoulder but was ethereally beautiful in a way no mortal woman would have been.

He blinked in confusion, not understanding her, and her gray eyes flashed in frustration.

"I warned you not to marry her," she clarified bluntly, stepping forward and placing her hands on her hips as if aggravated with him.

He blinked again in surprise, realizing she had indeed warned him against the disastrous marriage arranged by his family. He hadn't had a choice though. It was an excellent match on paper, both politically and monetarily advantageous, but it had been catastrophic in person.

Fortunately for him, after six long and painful years of avoiding one another, the shrew had run off with her lover and died almost instantly in a Roan attack on an outer colony. He felt slightly guilty at the enormous relief he'd felt upon the news of her death, but being left a young widower was far more preferable than a life of trying to forget he had a wife somewhere.

"I didn't have a choice," he answered, looking down into her upturned face. Her eyes were the soft gray of the Delsheni, and the pupils contracted to near nonexistence, indicating she was as deeply consumed by the Sight as he was.

He wondered if she was the ghost of an ancestor or, perhaps, she was simply someone sent by the gods to guide him. It wasn't unheard of. He had always assumed she was a goddess, but he had little faith left in goddesses and sprites and fairies. As an adult, his beliefs were far more practical. Yet there she was, as if living proof that the legends were real instead of pure mythology.

"What would you have me do?" he responded in an amused tone.

CHAPTER TWO

"You're supposed to marry me and keep me safe," she answered matter-of-factly.

He laughed outright at the absurd boldness of the idea.

She scowled. "I can't do it alone." She added in irritation, "It takes more than one."

"I'm afraid I'm a man who must live in the mortal word," he replied in the soft tone of an adult forced to dash the unrealistic dream of a girl. "Though I am pleased and privileged by your visits, I'm afraid I'm not a priest to spend his life in worship to a fairy goddess."

In response she simply frowned with impatience, and he wondered, with just a trace of dismay, if he'd now be permanently banned from her garden. He hoped not; he'd genuinely missed her and was pleased that she'd called to him again.

"I'm not a goddess," she contradicted firmly. "I'm as much flesh and blood as you. I've told you before: your only task in all these years is to find me before he does. You stopped looking for me, and now time is almost up."

"Before who does?" he asked gently. "A rival ghost perhaps? I'm afraid you do not exist in my world. Even this garden has not existed for more than a hundred years."

She frowned at him again, but this time in confusion. Turning, she regarded her surroundings critically, and, as she turned, the soft blue and purple echoes of days gone by began to melt like a watercolor painting left out in the rain. By the time she faced him again, they no longer stood among the ancient manicured trees and shrubbery, but in the ruins of a landscape neglected for more than three generations. It saddened him, for he preferred the dreamlike setting as it had been. She had changed too. Her hair had shortened from long, flowing tresses to a short bob, and her dress transformed from the elegant robes of the court to a strange, uniform-like garment that outlined her legs and exposed her arms.

"You're too late," she whispered in horror, the heartbreaking despair in her voice making him wish he could take his words back, to recreate the magic of the garden and the dream as it had always been.

Before he could answer, the distinct rumble of war machinery intruded, and there was no mistaking the advance of the armies he'd dedicated his entire life to fighting. It angered him. This was his vision, a longtime precious dream of childhood that he had held safe within his heart. The realities of adulthood and war had no place here.

"He's found me!" she cried in panic, throwing herself against him and clinging as if her life depended on it. "Don't let him take me!"

The action surprised him, and he stumbled backward slightly before stabilizing them both. The feel of her was not that of a cold shadow or illusion but intensely real and alive, confusing him all the more. No longer sure he was dreaming, he felt his body tense, his heart pounding. This was not the placid and amusing vision he'd anticipated. The Roan were very real and exceedingly dangerous. They had invaded every corner of the known human universe, and now they had invaded the quiet haven of his dreams. It was, however, no apparition that adhered to him in terror. She was warm and soft, and all of his preconceptions of her shattered as quickly as the dream-like park had melted away. Instinctively his arms closed around her, but just as quickly, she tore free as the thunder of explosions rumbled through them. He ducked reflexively from the anticipated heat of the explosions, then looked up to see that the Roan had disappeared. In their place were the even more terrifying armies of the Trogoul, a race dedicated to the total extinction of all humanity.

"Help me!" she cried over the roar of machinery, then turned and ran directly into the path of the advancing militia.

He shouted a warning and jolted forward, but, even as he did so, he felt the telltale signs that the vision was ending. It was like swimming through liquid glass. His feet and limbs were bogged down with an ethereal adhesive, forbidding movement. He roared in frustration, wanting the fragile connection to remain

CHAPTER TWO

intact, but no amount of determination on his part could maintain the connection.

When at last he reached her, it was too late. She lay sprawled and motionless across the torn lawn. He could do nothing except stare at her lifeless form in stunned horror as the dream pulled him upward toward consciousness. Then, with one last thunderous roar of machinery, the vision shattered and was gone.

He woke with a start, the recorded images of his family's long dead garden still projecting eerily across the wall of his living quarters in front of him. He knew, without any interpretation by the scribes, that the link to the vision would not return. The sense of loss was profound and overwhelming. He didn't want to let it go. He wanted to hold on, to go back, but the only thing that greeted his waiting mind was the silence of the room and the soft, ever-present rumble of the ship's engines. He waited a few more moments, hoping that his mind would feel the familiar pull, but nothing happened. A few seconds later, a soft chirping noise forced him fully awake. Opening his reader with a growl of frustration, he read the notification from the bridge: Malizore had been gravely wounded.

***

Kricket was aware of one thing: her head hurt. It was a bad dream, nothing more. A simple nightmare among many hauntings of her young mind. However, if that was so, she wondered why was it so god-awful painful to swallow. There was the unbearable pounding of her heartbeat torturing her mind with every pulse, but there were other sounds too: beeps, whistles, the sound of gas releasing from a valve. She was agonizingly tired and frozen with cold. She wanted to sleep, but something kept nagging at her, insisting she wake instead. It was irritating. Sleep promised peace, warmth, an escape to someplace quiet. A place with no invaders, no explosions, and no worries, but it was not to be. Her mind didn't want her to sleep. It wanted her to wake up; ready or not, she obeyed.

"She's awake!" William shouted in surprise as her lashes fluttered in the bright light of the medical bay. Then he grinned broadly in excitement when he noticed her wince at the sound. "She's awake!" he yelled again.

"I can see that," a female voice answered gently.

As the owner of the voice came closer into view, Kricket noticed she wasn't human, which fascinated her despite the painful throbbing in her head when she tried to focus her eyes. She had the shape of a human, was dressed in a uniform that might fit a human, but her face was anything but. It was difficult to describe at first, but that might have been because Kricket's vision was still blurred and the room around her seemed to sway up and down. The face, not unpleasant, was almost feline, but without the fur.

"You're a very lucky little girl, you know that?" the creature asked her kindly, as if she were speaking to a very young child. "How are you feeling?"

Kricket tried to answer but could only slowly move her lips; the sound refused to come.

The feline looked at her curiously for a moment, then analyzed a monitor next to her.

"You were given Ariker gas," she explained, as if that should make perfect sense. "Malizore broke your neck. The gas stimulates the repair. Sometimes, however...in humans," she paused, as if thinking, then looked back at her. "Sometimes it takes a little longer to wake up and for things like the vocal chords to start working. Then again," she added, smiling and showing a set of distinctly feline teeth, "your neck and throat were crushed, so that might produce swelling that would make your vocal chords difficult to use. I think we'll just have to counter it with a little Lanzalk and Tladlium in your meds, then watch and see. Sound good to you?"

Kricket nodded slightly as if she actually understood what was going on. She didn't know where she was, who the strange creature before her was, or why she was there. It briefly occurred to her that she could be dead, but that seemed too cruel a joke to

CHAPTER TWO

be real.

"She's all right?" another voice asked in a worried tone, and Kricket was surprised to see William's father approach. She hadn't seen him in weeks and had even accused her friend of lying that he was only on a business trip. She was sure the aliens had taken him.

"Yes, Professor. As I said, she's very lucky."

"Praise be," he murmured in his staccato way, wringing his hands as he paced in and out of Kricket's line of vision. "Leary and Irage must truly follow the child. Yes, yes, they must; how else does one explain it? Although I'm afraid it won't help her much, will it?"

"Probably not," the catlike creature answered kindly. "Try not to upset her with things right now, Professor. Let her rest. She's out of danger, but she still has several hours to go before she's feeling like herself again. There will be time enough to continue the war after she's recovered her strength a little."

Kricket turned her head to better focus in on William's father. She'd always liked him, although her mother had thought him irritating. He'd always reminded her of a tall, skinny, mad scientist, with a thick, white mass of tangled hair jutting out in all directions. His eyes were always wide open and huge, and he had the energy of ten rabbits, always bouncing, never still. Now though, he was as calm and subdued as she'd ever seen him. His large, worried eyes regarded her curiously, fingers fretting, as if he considered her the unexpected result of some kind of bizarre experiment.

"Poor girl," he said, coming closer to her and leaning down. "Always liked you." He rambled, nodding as he spoke. "I did. I really did. Never thought though, never in a million stars colliding; no, never."

"Father, please..." William said as he reached out and pulled the man back from the table a little. "Let her rest like Dr. Xnam says."

"Yes, yes," he answered fretfully. He moved away from her and then turned back, leaning uncomfortably close. "You did good, girlie," he said conspiratorially in a tumble of words. "You did more than good. They're very impressed, yes...very impressed. I've been answering questions about you for almost two days...which may in and of itself produce difficulties, but perhaps not. We'll simply have to see."

"Father..." William warned, eyes pleading with him to be silent.

"Ceya herself has ordered your background researched and your genes tested..." The Professor rambled, hand coming to his mouth as if considering a particularly complex equation. "You know what that means," he added, looking back at Kricket expectantly.

"Of course she doesn't, Father. How could she?"

William's father looked up in surprise, as if startled to see his son standing there, then slowly stood up and considered his words. "Perhaps not," he admitted, considering the possibility. "You know what it means, don't you, boy?"

"Yes, Father," he responded patiently, then turned to give her an encouraging smile. "You'll be fine, Kricket," he assured. "You've already survived the hardest part."

Kricket looked up at him with exhausted eyes. She was confused, scared, and cold. She assumed that she was in some kind of hospital, yet everything around her was strange and foreign. She didn't know why she was there and certainly didn't know why William and his father were there, although she was very glad of the their familiar faces. She wanted to go home, to forget the day had ever happened, but something in William's eyes kept her from trying to tell him so. He seemed relieved to see her wake up, but also terribly sad and extremely cautious. She had seen those cautious eyes before. She'd known him too long. They'd shared far too many secrets for her not to know that he was troubled and extremely worried.

"Where am I?" she asked, using tired and heavy fingers to silently motion signs in substitution for the words that her throat refused to speak, but William only frowned at her and looked away. She repeated the signs, but he only covered her hand with

CHAPTER TWO

his and cautiously looked around to see if anyone had noticed the movement. He must have decided they hadn't, because he sat back down next to her and held her hand, murmuring to her encouragingly yet not actually saying much of anything. That, perhaps, was the most telling. William wasn't one for shows of affection or excess chatter. People made him uncomfortable. He preferred his machines and computers and, although they were as close as siblings, he had never been one to hold her hand and pet it like a lost dog.

Deciding he was purposely choosing not to answer, yet still comforted by his presence, she closed her eyes and dozed a bit. Every once in a while, her eyes would flutter open. Each time William would be there by her side like a protective watchdog. His father would drift in and out of view, always fretting, checking the screens on the monitors around her, then disappearing again. The odd cat woman came several times and would readjust the settings if William's father changed them. She would give Kricket looks of deepest sympathy, as if she was very sorry for her, but she never asked questions or said much of anything. All the while, fatigue cocooned her like a thick blanket, preventing her from moving or even caring about the pain she felt. Then, all at once, William stood sharply, the movement jarring her awake. She hadn't realized she'd fallen soundly asleep, and it was disconcerting to wake up suddenly in the strange room, full of strange sounds and people.

"She'll live?" a new voice demanded curtly. She liked the sound of it, which was an odd thought, and the curiosity of it spurred her more fully awake. It was deep and clear and full of male authority. Looking up at William, she could see the anxiety in his face as he watched the newcomer with caution.

"Yes, Your Highness. She's strong, I told you. She's very strong. Yes, she most certainly is." William's father answered in his fretting way, wringing his hands as he spoke.

"I inquired of the doctor, Professor," the voice growled in reproof.

Kricket's brow knotted at the rudeness of it. William's hand tightened ever so slightly around hers as if he, too, disapproved, or perhaps he was somehow trying to shield her from it.

"She'll make a full recovery, Your Highness," the catlike doctor responded easily. "For the moment she's disoriented and frightened. The pain is under control, but full movement will still be difficult for a few more hours at best."

"Can she speak yet?"

"Yes, I believe so," the doctor answered patiently. "The swelling is down since this morning, and the repair almost complete."

"Does she know what she's done?" the new voice demanded.

"Not that I can tell," the doctor answered. "We'll know more as she recovers."

"Does she remember it?"

"I don't know, sir. I haven't asked. My current orders are to keep her alive and out of pain. The boy has remained by her side and has been conversing with her when she wakes."

At the doctor's reference to him, William stiffened, and she could almost hear him groan at becoming the center of attention. She squeezed his hand, and his head snapped in her direction, as if he'd forgotten she was there, then just as quickly turned back toward the newcomer.

"Well?" the voice demanded.

William swallowed thickly. "I haven't asked her...Your... Your Highness," he responded nervously.

There was no response for several long seconds, then the voice ordered brusquely, "Leave us."

William hesitated for the briefest of seconds, glancing at her cautiously, then began to step away. When she held on to his hand, he paused, then disentangled it and left her side. She was alone for a handful of seconds, the beeping and chirping of the computers blaring loudly in the now echoingly empty room around her. Before long, a tall figure made its way into the light around her bedside.

Her first thought was that he was not nearly as old as she'd expected him to be. He was actually quite young. That didn't

CHAPTER TWO

detract from the fact that he moved like someone who was used to being obeyed. The stern set to his jaw and the hardness in his dark brown eyes confirmed, more than anything else, the title he'd been addressed by.

Coltame paused briefly as he approached her bedside. He'd already suffered the shock of recognition on the recordings showing Malizore fall, already witnessed her lifeless and unconscious in the medical bay, already steeled himself against her for the second meeting, but he hadn't been prepared for the eyes. On the recordings, the eyelids had fluttered closed—exactly as they had in his vision. It had been agonizing to think he'd been too late, that Malizore had already killed her, but he'd buried the emotion deep within him as he watched them transfer her to the ship.

But how was a man supposed to react when his dreams molded into flesh and blood before him? No one prepared you for a thing like that. He didn't have the true gift of Sight that his maternal grandfather had. He couldn't pull useful information out of the air by merely asking for it or by staring in a reflective surface for hours on end. He was simply haunted by glimpses, colors, shadows, half-remembered thoughts…and by her. He'd known her practically all his life but never thought she was real. She existed only in his deepest dreams. She'd danced through the shadows of his nighttime thoughts since childhood. She was a fairy, a child goddess from beyond the gates of heavenly Annon, teasing him just out of reach of mortal boundaries. Yet, there she was, in living, breathing, flesh and blood, as if all his mind's conceptions had been factual recordings. It terrified him.

The large gray eyes that now regarded him shattered all previous efforts on his part to tell himself that he was mistaken. He had been able to rationalize that he had allowed the adrenaline of the moment, the shock and chaos that critical hour had produced, to fool himself. He assumed his mind had simply tricked him and transposed his deepest secret onto an unwitting little girl. But she was there—she was honestly there before him, regarding him just as curiously as she did in his dreams.

"How is it you're here?" he breathed in genuine wonder, stepping forward and hesitantly touching the light brown hair tussled across her forehead. His fingers slid down a tendril until it softly slid from his grasp. "How is it you're real?"

Kricket stared at the man, wide-eyed, wondering how anyone could shift from an aura of complete authority to such a soft and slightly pensive appearance in a matter of seconds. He was a handsome man, she decided, a little too old for her, but she could still admire him. He was tall and broad, with a figure and coloring that were flattered by his dark uniform. Thick, dark brown hair was pulled back tightly at his neck. The eyes that had been cold and almost black at his initial approach had softened into a deep, warm brown as he regarded her now.

"Are you a witch?" he asked, slowly sitting upon the stool at her bedside, all the while his eyes locking upon hers as if afraid she would disappear.

She frowned and dropped her eyes from his. It wasn't the first time someone had asked her that question. She was nothing, no more than a girl. However, strange things always seemed to happen around her—always had.

"Where did William go?" she asked, her voice raspy and strained, surprising her with its weakness. She looked back up and immediately wished that she hadn't. The softness in his eyes had vanished, and the black, cold, piercing look was instantly back in place.

"Is he your lover?" he snarled, surprising himself with the harshness of the words. He was not a covetous man where females were concerned; he had no need to be. The girl was no one to him, a local, one of many. What did he care if she had attached herself to the boy? Yet she was the image of his garden fairy. The little pixie was personal and dear, and the jealousy her words sparked surprised him. Something deep down inside him growled possessively at the thought that she might already have attached herself elsewhere.

"No," she answered, chuckling to herself. "I'm not exactly his type," she added with a soft whisper of a grin.

CHAPTER TWO

"Are you too brave for him?" he asked, mentally measuring her defiant stabbing of Malizore against the Professor's shy and uncertain son.

"Too female," she responded sleepily, eyes fluttering closed as a new round of pain medicine was automatically delivered to her system by the computer. When they lifted open again, it was obvious she was struggling with drug-induced grogginess.

Coltame regarded her curiously for a moment, the strange anger dissipating in lieu of the fascinating crumb of information she'd innocently offered about the Professor's only child. There were many cultural differences between her world and the ones he operated in, and there was a chance he could easily misinterpret her words.

"I'm cold," she murmured sleepily, closing her eyes and visibly shivering.

He stood and examined the monitors next to her bedside. They were placed at a lower setting, but not one that should have been uncomfortable. He was reluctant to change them in case the physicians had a good reason for keeping her body temperature down. On the other hand, if the girl was uncomfortable, it couldn't hurt to adjust it slightly. Reaching up, he increased the thermostat to a level he would have found comfortable and noticed her muscles almost instantly relax against the firm surface of the table.

"Do you know who I am?" he asked, returning to the original reason for his visit.

She shook her head, lazily succumbing to the drowsiness now that the temperature of the table began to warm the chill from her body. William had called him "Your Highness," although the significance of that meant nothing to her.

"You don't recognize me? Not even a little?" he asked, unable to keep the disappointment out of his voice.

She turned and observed him more closely, actively fighting the sleep that threatened to take her back to pleasant unconsciousness.

Seeing the deepening glaze in her eyes, he stood and lowered the temperature of the bed once again. In response, she seemed to wake a little and blinked at him lazily as he resumed his seat.

"You have the same eyes," she answered distantly, still drifting from the medications she'd been given.

"The same eyes as what?" he asked, hopeful that she recognized him too, that perhaps she had some answer to how she had slipped from his visions and into mortal life.

"Malizore," she answered softly, remembering William's name for the thug who'd choked her. Then she frowned deeply in confusion at the look of murderous rage that crossed his face. It was frightening, and she wished she could take it back.

"My father's illegitimate half brother," he responded coldly, causing her to wince visibly. "I assure you the family resemblance ends there."

"I'm sorry," she answered, and she genuinely was. "My mom always says we can't choose our relatives. If we could, we'd all be a lot happier."

Coltame sat back on his stool and regarded her darkly. She was heavily medicated, and he doubted her comment had been meant to offend. Malizore was a pirate; no family would ever be proud of those ties. He was also deeply disappointed she didn't recognize him. He had hoped... *What had I hoped?* he wondered silently to himself. *I had hoped my fairy had come to life,* he thought bitterly. *A last, fragile wish that life could be a little nicer than it actually is. A hope that is best buried with the rest of my childish desires*, he silently chastised.

"We will speak again when you have recovered," he pronounced, standing abruptly.

She didn't respond, just watched him with her large eyes. He stood there, mesmerized by them for several long seconds before forcing himself to turn and stride purposely from the room. He burst through the doorway, temper high and full of frustration, and stormed down the hallway without acknowledging the medical staff patiently waiting to resume their duties.

He didn't stop until he reached his private quarters, barreling inside and locking the door with more force than was necessary.

CHAPTER TWO

Only once inside did he allow his emotions free. He grabbed the first thing his hand could reach and slammed it violently into the wall, where it thudded with an echoing thwack, sliding helplessly to the floor. It was a stupid lack of self-control, but what else was he supposed to do? The girl had been ripped right out of his daydreams. Was it a plot? Had she been genetically created and planted into his life simply to unnerve him? He had told no one besides the scribes and his cousin. It was a private, carefully guarded, secret. A small vestige of peace and happiness in a life condemned to war and the duplicitous intrigue of court. Yet the girl had come to life and had wounded the pirate king more severely than any mechanized fighter had been able to. All sources indicated she hadn't killed him, but that didn't matter. The ferocity of it assured she would be catapulted into legend.

No one had been able to stop Malizore; he was a legend in his own right. He was called "The Unstoppable," yet the girl had not only immobilized him, she'd emasculated him. Malizore's court had been quick to dispel the reports he had been fully castrated, simply wounded, but he had seen the recordings of it from the battle computers. All of the angles had been meticulously analyzed and the possible results hotly debated. A man's masculinity was everything to him—his identity. If it was true, and Malizore still lived, he would be shamed and dishonored beyond comprehension.

Coltame exhaled deeply, forcing his anxieties to exhale along it. The girl needed protection. She was a child, not a warrior, and Malizore wouldn't remain wounded for long. His minions would move quickly to reduce the damage done by the release of images showing him weak and falling from the wound inflicted by her. They would retaliate, and he needed to make sure she was well protected when they did. The gods had said so.

Long-term protection was the difficult problem. He would have to find a way to ensure her security long after public adulation and fleeting celebrity had left her. His hand came to his mouth, and he paced as he considered the feasibility of his options. If he made it known that she was under his protection, it would be assumed that she was his mistress. She was not only too young for that, which would bring unwanted scandal to his doorstep, but her instant fame at being the only one in ages to seriously wound Malizore would make her too valuable. Whether she was a warrior by trade or not, she would now have the status of one, and her honor would need to be respected and guarded. Society would demand that she be a man's wife, not a mistress.

The idea of handing her over to another man in marriage inexplicably caused him to feel a deep and primal possessiveness that confused him. He had no explanation for it other than he simply wanted to keep her for himself. If his first wife had lived, he would have had little difficulty in taking her as a second, but he could never consider her for a first. He was a grandson of the emperor; his family was already negotiating his next alliance. They would demand a pristine bloodline in his next mate, not a colonial mixed blood who would place mongrel offspring in a position close to the throne.

Was the girl really his fairy? Was she truly sent by gods he'd long ago dismissed as simple fantasy? The idea was preposterous, yet there she was, in living flesh.

In his vision, the fairy had said he was to marry her, but the girl was a colonist with no bloodline. His family would never allow it. Yet if he didn't protect her from Malizore, who would? Who could have enough power to keep the girl safe? She couldn't remain on her own without a family to protect her. Some sort of union was going to have to be arranged for her...So why not him? He had the power, influence, and finances to keep her safe. If the gods had sent her to him, wasn't there a case for divine intervention? His head began to ache as he contemplated his father's response to the idea.

The best thing to do, the most sensible thing to do, would be to send her back to an academy in the Delsheni sector of space, but he simply didn't want to. She was his vision come to life. His fairy, his goddess. The possessiveness he felt was overwhelming. She had been sent to him—he had no doubt

CHAPTER TWO

about it—and what was his was not going to be relinquished easily.

There was always the possibility that he could capitulate and take on the female his father and grandfather were lobbying for. If he made the powers that be happy enough, then perhaps he could marry the girl he wanted afterward with little protest. He shuddered involuntarily at the thought. He had done his duty to his family the first time by accepting the wife they had chosen for him and was loathe to do so again. He paused and thought of the pretty little sprite in the garden. He hadn't had a vision of her for nearly six years, until the precise morning she came to life on the planet below him. That couldn't be a coincidence. Had it truly been a vision of what was to come? He hadn't thought he was that talented.

One thing was certain, the girl had been shown to him not once but many times over the course of his lifetime. The gods he claimed to have so very little faith in had tried their best to inform him that she was coming, then delivered her into his care. They had decreed that she was his responsibility, and he alone would assume the role of her protector. *But how*? He closed his eyes and leaned his head back in a silent plea for direction. He had no faith left in the gods and goddesses his mother's people worshiped. He was a man of the world in which he lived, his father's world; perhaps that was why they refused to answer him.

CHAPTER THREE

"You sent for me?" Coltame asked brusquely as he approached the Redan physician. He had known the feline most of his life; she was one of the few people he actually trusted. In the power-hungry world of his grandfather's court, more family members died from poison alone than any other form of death; having a trusted physician was critical. She had followed him home when he returned to the Rheigan capitol as a boy and managed to keep him in excellent health until he could return to his uncle's ship. In gratitude he'd placed her in a position to aid him when necessary.

"You asked to be informed if anything strange happened during the girl's treatment," Xnam replied, and, when he nodded, she motioned for him to follow her.

They walked across the now deserted room to a small console, where she typed a series of patterns, illuminating several small screens. "I sent the boy back to his father's quarters to rest while I put her through decontamination again," she said absently.

"Did she need it?" he asked, concern for the girl jumping to the forefront of his thoughts. It wasn't unusual for locals of a

CHAPTER THREE

third-class world, or even colonists on a sanctioned colony, to need decontaminating from the local bacteria and viruses that inhabited natural environments, but rare to have to endure the process twice.

"No," she replied. "It was an excuse. I didn't want him in here when you returned."

Coltame paused and digested the information she supplied. "You think he's a spy?" he asked seriously. Spies were always a concern. He was a senior ranking grandson of the reigning emperor. There were many who would pay a great deal to know what he did while he was away from court—even more who would pay dearly to see him never return.

"I think he's more loyal to the girl than to the father," she responded bluntly, giving him a significant look.

"You think they're lovers?" he asked, doing an unusually poor job of masking his expression.

Xnam noted the reaction curiously, filing it away for future reference. Possessiveness was a well-documented Rheigan trait, but she had yet to see it the young prince. The girl was an odd choice for him, but, given her almost overnight rise to fame for stabbing the pirate king, perhaps it wasn't too unusual. She would certainly have plenty of suitors once she was introduced into mainstream society.

Turning from him, she sniffed in amusement, then shook her head. Knowing the current, and, in her opinion, antiquated social laws restricting human relationships, she didn't dare express her opinions until she could confirm them.

"No," she answered truthfully. "The boy is protective and obviously emotionally bonded to her, but the loyalty seems more born of friendship or possibly some sort of foster-sibling relationship."

Coltame nodded and relaxed a little. He wondered again at the girl's earlier comment about being too female to attract the boy's attentions, then dismissed the thought as the physician pulled up what looked suspiciously like genetic scans.

"Are you familiar with Redan VHT genetic mapping?" she

asked, knowing, even as she formed the words, that he was. Coltame, at his heart, was a far better scientist than he was a politician. Many hoped, if his family line stayed in power, that the scientific community would flourish a little better under his influence.

He nodded silently and waited for her to continue.

"Ceya asked for a standard ESU map on the girl. She was found in the middle of a known colony, not to mention the Professor himself knows her. She's definitely older than she appears, but right now the captain has no grounds for not returning her to her family other than we're worried Malizore might retaliate."

"Malizore will retaliate," he corrected.

She nodded to him in agreement. "But apparently the mother wants her back," she countered.

"How did she find out we have her?" he asked, frowning. The technology of the planet below was rudimentary at best. It should be easy for her to disappear and simply be considered a casualty; at least, he'd been hoping it would be easy.

"The Professor..." she answered, giving him a disgruntled look.

"The Professor?" he countered.

"Apparently he's well acquainted with the family and took it upon himself to assure the mother that she was all right and would be returned," she clarified, unable to keep a slight sourness from tingeing her words.

Coltame swore in several languages at the breach of protocol. The Professor was technically in hiding and under their protection after an attempt by the Roan forces to capture him. Not only had he exposed himself to a local as still present on the outpost, but, by bypassing official channels, he had effectively informed whatever Roan spies were lurking about that the girl had survived as well. Secreting her away would be far more difficult now.

The physician nodded in agreement. She had her own concerns with the elusive Professor DeSirpi, but, until she had

CHAPTER THREE

proof, she'd hold her tongue. "If Ceya can prove the girl is attached to the colony the Professor was involved with, then she can trace the girl's family to a Federated world—"

"And to a registered family member who we can encourage to step forward and intercede on her behalf," Coltame finished. It made perfect sense. The girl couldn't be returned and expected to live more than a few hours. Malizore's forces would already be mobilizing to make a very public example of her.

"The reason I called for you though," she began, redirecting the conversation, "is that I ran the ESU but also thought it prudent, since I have the proper technology with me, to run a VHT. I didn't tell anyone I had taken additional samples for the extra test."

He nodded in understanding. She either hadn't wanted anyone to know she had the rare and, in most cases, forbidden, Redan equipment on board a Federation ship, or she hadn't wanted the results tampered with. "What did you find out?" he asked, his curiosity tweaked.

"Here are the results of the ESU," she answered, gesturing to the screens in front of them.

He glanced over the display without bothering to hide his disappointment. The girl was obviously a local mongrel, without any desirable markers, and he found nothing to suggest that she could have descended from any of the known lines. If anything, based on the data in front of him, many of her genes either were highly undesirable or carried potentially unhealthy traits.

"Not exactly pretty is it?" he commented, the disappointment thick in his voice. There was no way he could consider marrying her—even as a second wife. At best, he might be able to risk public displeasure and keep her as a mistress, but he was loath to do so.

"On first glance, no, not all…But this isn't her sample," Xnam answered, waiting for his reaction and stifling an amused look when his eyes popped up in surprise. It was entertaining to watch him try to suppress his interest in the girl. Then again, extreme ferocity was well admired by the Rheigans. Perhaps his

Rheigan blood found her attack on Malizore to be irresistible.

"What?" he asked, double checking the identification bars attached to the results.

"That's exactly what I asked," she answered, giving him another significant look. "I've been paying attention to the VHT, double and triple checking what I found. When I went to pull the ESU, I was dumbfounded by the discrepancies. So I ran it again."

"And?" he pressed.

"When the second ESU came out identical to the first, I pulled the computer board apart and found this," she said, opening her hand to display a tiny device, no larger than a small flea, encased in a clear container. "It's a cryptor. I haven't seen one in ages. It'll burrow its way into a board and absorb any information the computer puts out. It then retransmits only what its installer wants to be displayed on the screen."

"I've heard of them," he responded, frowning. "But never heard of one getting onto a military ship."

"You can't get them on board," she insisted. "The scanners specifically search for them each and every time someone's brought in—no exceptions. These things can be deadly if you're heading into battle and your computers aren't giving you the right information."

"Then how did it get here?" he asked, brows knotting even tighter. Delsheni battleships were enormous, requiring tens of thousands of crew as well as housing an entire civilian city of family members and support staff. Something like a cryptor was a serious breach of security.

"Someone had to have the knowledge, and equipment, to build it after they'd arrived," she answered. "It's not an easy device to create. You have to have specialized tools and a broad knowledge of the security systems on the computer you're trying to tap."

"The Professor."

"That was my initial thought, but, as usual, I have absolutely no proof," she confirmed with just a hint of frustration.

CHAPTER THREE

"But why?"

"This," she replied, closing the data on the original screen and displaying a new set of ESU results, along with the less familiar VHT.

"She's blood," Coltame breathed softly in surprise. He blinked hard and then reread the data on the screen, dumbfounded by the disparity of the results.

"Not just any blood," Xnam confirmed, nodding at his reaction. "She's got a better genetic chart than you. You don't see scans like this in younger generations. Not since laboratory reproduction and artificial birthing tanks were outlawed. That was over sixty years ago. The Professor is hiding her, I'm sure of it, but I'm not positive I know why yet."

"You don't think the Professor's migration to the colony was a ruse, do you? Was his real aim to return to laboratory purebreds without the government knowing?"

"It's not just Delsheni royal blood. Look here," she said, pointing to several markers and suppressing a triumphant grin as he blanched.

"Rheigan," he confirmed, recognizing genetic markers of the current imperial family that would have been proudly displayed on any other female's charts.

"Blood Rheigan," she confirmed, indicating the current royal line: his line.

"That doesn't solve the mystery of how she was found in a backwater colony," he muttered, head spinning. Echoes of his visions spun through his head. She had to be the girl the gods were telling him to find. For someone who had given up his faith in deities and their mysticism, it was a startling and intensely disconcerting realization. He had asked for divine intervention, and now it was staring him in the face.

"Which Delsheni house is she most closely associated with?"

"That's what I wanted to have solved before I called you," she admitted.

"And have you?"

"Nothing definitive," she answered, shaking her head. "But

until now, I was more interested in her maternal side. The problem is that the Professor's already pulled a copy of the fake ESU to take to Ceya and the captain. I think you need to give them a heads-up that the data he's about to feed them isn't accurate."

"I'll call now and tell them that I need to meet about a serious breach of security," he said. "The captain will be more concerned with that than the girl."

She nodded curtly in agreement, then added, "You can tell them I've narrowed down the options of her paternity, but they'll be more interested in the identification of her maternal line."

"Who?" he asked, not bothering to hide his eager curiosity.

"Paternally, she almost has to have a Delsheni sire, even if she's lab bred. The markers are too pronounced. She's definitely related within three generations to the former Emperor Azill."

Coltame nodded. He was also related to the former emperor through his mother's line; that wasn't unusual. Azill had been a Delsheni pacifist and, as such, had not lasted long on the throne before his father's family, a family of Rheigan warlords, had overthrown him. In exile, however, he had continued to live a long life and had produced far more children than the two sons he formally recognized. Half the known universe seemed to claim him as an ancestor.

"And the Rheigan markers?" he asked, curious to know those results. That would be the true test. If she was a blood relative to his grandfather, the current grand emperor, there would be no questioning the right of the empire to take her away from the colony and place her within a suitable household.

She nodded in affirmation, eyes twinkling and allowing herself a wide, catlike grin. "Hollin," she said simply, grinning more broadly as his eyes widened.

"Are you positive?" he asked, stunned to hear a name straight out of legend.

"He was one of the last of your grandfather's generation to be genetically bred," she confirmed. "He inherited several markers from his dame that were unique to his line. A line which was

CHAPTER THREE

obliterated after the last uprising. The girl has all of them. It's a ninety-nine percent positive identification through the maternal line. I've run the sample three times."

Coltame closed his eyes and leaned against the console. Hollin had been his grandfather's half brother. There were many people of influence who had wanted him on the throne over the current emperor, but two separate attempts to grab the title had failed, and Hollin had simply vanished. If Xnam was correct, the girl's existence would solve one of the longest-running mysteries of modern time.

"She's older than I initially thought," Xnam continued, "about the same age as the Professor's son, which puts her just past her majority. There's something else you should know," Xnam said quietly, bringing him back from his musings. "She's healed too quickly. She shouldn't have survived, yet now I doubt there'll be a mark on her by morning."

"What do you think is going on?" he asked. "Do you think the Professor was experimenting with enhancing genomes?"

Xnam shrugged and shook her head, unwilling to venture beyond the realm of scientific fact. "Her revidification markers are off the chart," she said at last.

"Revidification markers? You mean that she's been exposed to an Annonian crystal?" he asked cautiously. Annonian crystals were a rare and much sought after source of energy. Even the smallest stones had been known to power entire cities for generations. That would certainly explain Malizore's interest in the colony beyond basic territorial expansion. A new source of energy crystals would be profitable enough to tempt anyone to the outskirts of society.

Xnam shrugged again, unwilling to speculate. It was more than that. If the girl had simply been exposed latently, there would be a gradual decline in exposure markers that could be mapped. There was no indication that she'd been removed. It was as if she was still experiencing direct exposure, which simply didn't make sense.

"Weren't the keys to Hollin's Guardian said to originate with an older form of power crystals?" she asked speculatively. "Hollin was—"

"You're on dangerous ground, Doctor," he replied simply, his face impassive.

Talk of the Emperor's half brother had been forbidden for decades, but it was widely speculated upon. If you were Delsheni, then Hollin, with his great war machine, was a hero of mythical proportions. But if you were Rheigan, he was a traitor. Coltame descended from both lines and had a strong appreciation for both versions of history, but he was still his grandfather's representative to the outer regions. He would publicly maintain the party line at all times.

"I'll continue to monitor her," Xnam said simply, silently admitting that she'd continue to probe into the mystery.

***

Kricket shifted restlessly in her induced sleep. She didn't want to sleep, but her body wouldn't respond to her commands to wake up. It was a disconcerting feeling, to be wide awake and asleep at the same time. The feeling was enough to drive her mad.

Part of it was that she knew what was going to happen. The signs were all there: the warming sensation, the energy surge accelerating her pulse. She was too exhausted to fight it and, in the end, relaxed her will and let it overtake her. Her eyes opened, pupils constricted, as the Sight overtook her. The lights of the medical bay swirled past her, and, within seconds, she was back in the garden.

There wasn't much left. The invaders had come, just as she'd foreseen on her last visit. And they'd destroyed it—just like they would try to destroy her.

CHAPTER FOUR

"So you're saying Hollin came here?" Captain Jaget asked skeptically. Although difficult to believe, the idea rubbed at him with a grain of truth. Where better to disappear than the middle of nowhere? It seemed his mission was far more complicated than he'd suspected.

He was the captain of an older, but still powerful, warship, and yet his assignment, by imperial command, was to go out far beyond the border of insignificance and irrelevant to ferry home a mad scientist to the Rheigan capital—all on the whim of an aging and senile emperor. He'd been disgruntled to have been taken off the battlefront, where he could offer shelter and protection to the troops still battling the Trogoul, only to find himself in the middle of a Roan invasion and Malizore himself on the front lines. If Coltame was correct, his seemingly innocuous mission was far more critical to the interests of the empire than he could have previously speculated.

Jaget rubbed his face roughly with his thick fingers. Although well past middle age, he was still a strong man. Nothing about his assignment made sense. There was only so much he could chalk up to Rheigan distrust and misuse of the Delsheni fleet.

"I believe Hollin not only spent his exile on this colony, I think he might have set up operations there," Coltame answered, his face stern and regal, yet just a trace of bright excitement shining in his eyes. The legend of Hollin brought back too many childhood memories. There wasn't a Delsheni boy alive who didn't dream of finding Hollin and his brave band of warriors, of resurrecting the Guardian and restoring the Delsheni Empire. He might be only half Delsheni, but the allure of Hollin's legend was embedded deep within his heart. "I think that's what lured the Professor here, and I'm sure that's why Malizore himself is involved."

"Do you believe the Professor is an agent of the empire? Or is he working alone?" Ceya asked. Her brother might have missed the twinkle in her son's eyes, but she hadn't. It pleased her to see she hadn't ingrained her society's culture in her son vainly. He was his father's heir and had to live in his father's world, but he Coltame was her child too; Jaget needed to remember that.

"The empire...or Malizore," Coltame added bluntly. At his uncle's sharp intake of breath, he added, "A cryptor was inserted into the medical facility's main board. The ship's security scans everyone for cryptors upon arrival. So whoever inserted it not only had to have the knowledge to build it but the opportunity to insert it. This particular device was designed specifically to hide the genetic background of the girl—a girl whose genetic map seems to indicate laboratory precision and whose revidification markers are, according to Dr. Xnam, off the charts. He's hiding her. I know it."

Jaget sat back in his oversized chair and stroked his graying goatee absently as he absorbed the information his nephew presented. Even now, the idea of stumbling upon Hollin's secret encampment made his heart skip a beat. He was not prone to fancy. He was a career military man who had built his life around facts and routine. Although the current Rheigan doctrine stated the Guardian had never existed, that it was no more than a weapon built by Hollin to resemble the legendary robot and put

CHAPTER FOUR

fear into the hearts of Trogoul, he knew that it had been real.

"I don't know if I ever told you," he began slowly and in a thoughtful voice. "But when I was very, very young, long before your mother was born, the Trogoul attacked our planet."

Coltame closed his eyes slowly in an effort to refocus his thoughts, caught off guard by his uncle's sudden switch in tone. Since his return, things had been tense at best between them. It was well known that there was no love lost between the Delsheni and the Rheigans. He genuinely grieved the loss of his uncle's trust. Coltame had-had no choice, though. His father had formally recognized him as his son, the Emperor himself had formally recognized him as one of his grandsons, and the ramification of that was a return to the royal court to learn his place in society.

"After days and days of fire and destruction, the city fell, and the Trogoul forced everyone into what had been the center marketplace. I don't need to tell you what we faced there," Jaget continued, voice distant as he reminisced.

Coltame nodded solemnly. The Trogoul didn't take prisoners. They might take strong and healthy men to work the mines on oxygenated planets, but, for the most part, they simply slaughtered their enemies en masse and recycled their bodies into the food chain. It was hideous and gruesome, but, to the Trogoul, it was a religious ceremony of victory that honored their gods.

"I was painfully young, but I will never forget it. The despair, the hopelessness of everyone around me. Everything was destroyed or on fire. We had lost everything: our home, our lands, our way of life. And then, just as twilight descended upon us, the Guardian emerged like a sentinel knight sent straight from the high pillars of Annon."

Coltame sat up straight at the mention of the Guardian. Firsthand testimony of the robot was forbidden, and, in all the stories of his youth, his uncle had never mentioned he'd seen it personally. He was fascinated and not only thrilled to meet an actual eye witness but delighted that his uncle would confide in him a family secret. For the captain to mention it, knowing that he was an agent of his grandfather, could very well result in the stripping of his command. Perhaps his uncle was willing to trust him again after all.

"I will never forget that moment," Jaget continued, eyes closing as if seeing the memory again in his mind's eye. "I will never forget that I owe Hollin and his crew a debt of life and freedom that can never be repaid."

He opened his eyes and regarded his nephew frankly. "So do you. It was during that liberation that my mother met her second husband: your mother's father." He paused briefly, then asked, "You're positive that this girl is Hollin's descendant?"

"Dr. Xnam reports that she has genetic markers unique to that line, which don't exist anymore. She says the Redan VHT genetic mapping positively identifies her paternally as Azill's issue within three generations and maternally as Hollin's offspring within two generations," Coltame answered.

"Redan VHT genetic mapping is illegal," Jaget responded flatly.

"So is an eyewitness account of the Guardian," his nephew countered in the same tone, and was rewarded by a slight twitch of his uncle's lips upward into a small, bemused smile.

"So the question before us now is what to do with her," Ceya interjected. Her son's fascination with the girl surprised her. She knew he'd been to visit her in the medical bay more than once; now he was revealing that he'd had his personal physician run specific genetic testing on her. As a grandson of the emperor, he was the official Rheigan presence on the ship, and she wondered how much he had known about her in advance of her sudden appearance with the Professor's son.

"There are many questions before us, the least of which is the girl," Jaget responded gruffly. "The Professor is accused of knowingly building a forbidden device and tampering with a military computer—be it only a medical computer. Malizore has been seriously wounded. Now we learn that Hollin's encampment is possibly down on the surface. If this is so, then it

CHAPTER FOUR

stands to reason that the Guardian itself could be hidden somewhere close. No, there is much more here than what to do with the girl."

"I think answers are with the girl," Coltame replied. When the eyes of the room centered back on him, he added, "Hollin apparently came to this world when he fled from the emperor. His descendants, as proven by the girl's existence, are still here. Her revidification markers are off the charts, indicating that she's been directly exposed to a specific crystal power source—one rumored to have been associated with the Guardian robot. The Professor is willing to go to extreme measures to hide her from us, even though we're here by order of the emperor himself. The Professor," he stressed, "who is considered the galaxy's foremost expert on robotic warfare. Someone who has held the emperor's favor for decades, yet chose to give up his life's work and retreat to a colony devoid of technology—a colony that just happens to harbor Hollin's descendants. Descendants who just might know where their patriarch hid the Guardian robot—the most powerful war machine in the entire galaxy."

"What are you saying?" Ceya asked, brow creasing slightly.

"I'm saying I think the emperor knew where Hollin was all along. I think he sent DeSirpi to infiltrate his camp; didn't the Professor's father supposedly work with a tertiary team of scientists assigned to the Guardian project?"

Jaget nodded slowly in confirmation, stroking his goatee again as he considered the possibilities being presented. Speculating on the motive of the emperor was dangerous grounds. One had to walk carefully, even around the most innocuous of situations.

"I believe he sent the Professor to ingratiate himself with Hollin's family and discover the secrets of the Guardian. Malizore probably figured out that's what he was up to. The temptation alone would have been too much for him to resist. Even the remote possibility of securing the Guardian for the Roan would be worth the risks of a trip here. I think the girl might have the key to the information everyone is searching for. What we have to do is hold on to her long enough for her to trust us and tell us what we need to know."

Jaget raised a silver eyebrow at his sister's son, wondering if the boy realized he was voicing treason. He was the emperor's grandson, one of many to be sure, but, as such, he owed total loyalty and obedience to his grandsire. If the girl were so important, his first duty, as the sole Rheigan authority on the ship, was to confiscate the child and send her packing to court, not put the Delsheni in a position to utilize her. Coltame was no fool; he'd spent too many years at court not to know how to walk the party line. Perhaps there was hope that the boy hadn't had all of his Delsheni blood beaten out of him after all.

"But then why sabotage the medical computers? He would have far more to gain by exposing the girl's ancestor," Ceya interjected. "Three quarters of the known universe would rejoice that Hollin survived."

"And three quarters of the universe would gain new hope that they could stand up to the Rheigan Empire." Jaget countered. "The Professor might be Delsheni, but his loyalties have always been embedded with the Rheigans…no offense," he added gruffly, nodding but not looking at his nephew. "He's most likely shielding her and her family from anyone's notice until the robot—or the robot's power source—is secure. The girl's presence will raise too many eyes in this direction; there's too great a chance that the wrong forces will find the robot and secure it before the empire does."

"Or he's playing many sides at once, and the girl might reveal his hands," Coltame supplied, which, given the history of the man, was not implausible. "He broke protocol and contacted the girl's mother, promising he'd return her safely. There is no logical reason for him to do that except, perhaps, the woman is Hollin's daughter and he needs to stay in her favor. Perhaps Hollin himself is still alive. Who knows? Dr. Xnam says the girl's sire is most likely of Delsheni royal blood. That suggests there's more in play here than we're privy to. Malizore tried to

CHAPTER FOUR

kill the girl, so he's unaware, we assume, of her lineage, but I'll bet my place in the royal hierarchy he knows the Professor was here trying to dig up the Guardian."

"So you think the emperor knows the Guardian is here too?" Ceya asked. "Then why send a Delsheni warship to the rescue? Why not a Rheigan battle cruiser?"

"Talk of the Sentinel Guardian is forbidden," Coltame speculated. "If it doesn't exist, diverting a Rheigan ship from the front might expose that it does. I assume he hopes it's here and, if it is, wants it secured before the Delsheni or Malizore or even the Trogoul realize it's here. Obviously it's not a simple task. The Professor has been here for over two decades," he added. He was on dangerous ground, but present at the family meeting were only his mother and his uncle. More importantly, it was not being recorded for the official log.

"Even if she'd been a local, I wouldn't have returned her," Jaget said, surprising his nephew. At Coltame's curious look, he added, "She committed an act of unparalleled bravery…even if it was accidental. Given the background we've already dug up on her, though, that seems less and less likely. I had planned to send her to the Academy; the Delsheni can always use good people, and the military doesn't pay as much heed to bloodlines as others do. No, sending her back to the planet she came from would be a death sentence. Malizore will never let her live. I doubt he'll even let her family live."

"What had you discovered about her?" Coltame asked, unable to help himself.

Jaget worked his jaw a bit, reluctant as the ship's captain to answer, but he enjoyed the easiness in which the confidential conversation was flowing and was reticent to break it with more distrust. Coltame seemed to allude, despite his exterior manner, that he might not be as anti-Delsheni as the party line demanded he be. He hoped so; he'd missed him. It was still dangerous ground. There was no quarter with Rheigans. They took distinct, and often perverted, pleasure in tearing their enemies apart.

"Apparently she's been quite involved with the local

resistance to the Roan. From what we can tell, she's been active in sabotaging their operations, planting primitive explosives to blow up their supply lines, things like that. Nothing highly advanced, mind you, but disruptive nonetheless. She also apparently holds some sort of high ranking in a form of close contact hand-and-foot combat similar to the Nubalah; so she's not the innocent little child she appears to be."

Coltame couldn't hide the surprise on his face; his eyes even found their way to the two Nubalah warriors guarding the door. They were considered one of the most effective bodyguards in the known universe and not something that he would like to tangle with.

"But that form of combat isn't unheard of in other human races," his uncle continued casually. "If she's Hollin's granddaughter, then it probably isn't unusual that the family educated her in such things and insisted she know how to defend herself—with or without the use of weapons or machinery."

"So..." Ceya interjected softly. "The question seems to be, what to do with her now? Return her to her mother?"

"Hardly," Jaget answered back gruffly. "We find her sire. You never know what you'll find when you go looking for genetic links. The royal lines are hopelessly interbred. We'll most likely be able to attach her almost anywhere we like. We simply search the family tree and find a branch capable of protecting her from Malizore. It shouldn't be too hard. She's young, of good blood, and every information outlet in the galaxy is proclaiming her heroic attack on Malizore. The general population is already rabid in their fascination with her and demanding to know more as soon as possible. Her blood connection to Hollin will be a liability in Rheigan waters, but an asset just about everywhere else. No, I don't think it will be hard to place her."

"Why a liability to the Rheigans?" Coltame asked before he could stop himself. Now was not the time to disclose his thoughts of keeping the girl for himself, but her placement would undoubtedly affect the ease of his eventually carrying out

CHAPTER FOUR

those plans.

"Because Hollin was declared a traitor by the emperor," Jaget rebutted testily, looking at his nephew as if the boy had gone mad. "I doubt you'll find many in that camp willing to acknowledge their links to his lineage."

Ceya regarded her son curiously as he struggled with the emotions that crossed his young face. It had to be hard on him: To be reared Delsheni, only to be claimed by the Rheigans. To have a foot in both worlds, yet never be fully trusted by either. She felt for him. She could tell he was as fascinated by Hollin's legend as any Delsheni, yet he was Rheigan and had to assume the party line that Hollin was no more than a con artist out to dupe the universe into thinking he'd resurrected a mythical guardian of old. Whether it was a scam or not, whether the robot existed or was simply a machine created to look like it, Hollin had saved them from the Trogoul; no one could deny that. His only sin was in having the bravery to stand up to the emperor and refuse to use that same machine to suppress the masses, which, in the opinion of many, was no sin at all.

***

"Injudiciousness…" the Professor muttered under his breath. He squirmed restlessly in his seat in the waiting area outside the captain's conference room. "Foolishness…lack of prudence, yes…That's all it is."

All he had to do was hand over the girl's genetic scans, and they'd lose interest in her fast enough. Margaret was furious with him, and that was never a good thing. The girl's mother, like her father before her, was not a force to be taken lightly. The boy should have known better than to keep his associations with her. Malizore went directly for him, and the boy had led them right to the girl. What a muddle things had become.

"Imprudence…naiveté, thoughtlessness…Injudicious—that's the word for it. No judgment, no thinking…"

Despite his resolve to stay calm, he jumped up and began to

pace. The sooner he got the girl back to her mother, the better. Margaret was furious, and who knew what she was capable of while in the throes of her high temper.

He stopped suddenly, turning to glare at the closed doors that refused him entrance. He was so damn close, and this was going to ruin everything. Blood son or not, the boy was an idiot. All he'd had to do was stay shut up in the shelter, but no, he had gone outside, and Malizore had spotted him as quickly as a purple duck on a white sand dune.

If the emperor heard word of the girl's existence before Senator Cronus was ready to reveal his hand, it was game over for all of them. That simply couldn't be allowed. There was no way to start again—there was no time, not with what was fast approaching. All he had to do was stay calm, get the girl back to Margaret, and then convince the captain that it was time to take him back to Syphlein before all hell broke loose.

"Injudiciousness..." he muttered irritably, then turned to continued his agitated pacing.

***

Kricket sat up, or, rather, tried to sit up, but the result was a little messy and left her teetering unsteadily on the narrow platform of the medical bed.

"Hold on. You're not nearly ready to get up and about," William fretted, stabilizing her and trying to encourage her to lie back down.

"I want to go home," she spat defiantly, too tired and achy to even try and smooth out her temper. She was done with the medical bay, with being poked and prodded and stared at.

"That's not going to possible for a while," he answered, sighing heavily when she refused to allow him to push her backward.

"Why the hell not?" she demanded irritably, forehead knotted tightly in a deep frown.

"Because you're healing nicely, but you're still seriously

CHAPTER FOUR

hurt," Dr. Xnam replied sweetly, as if that was the most obvious answer.

"I'm fine," Kricket insisted crossly, eyes defiant.

"You'll be fine when I decide that you're fine," Xnam responded in a firm tone. "Now, are you going to be a good girl and lie back down, or am I going to sedate you into unconsciousness again? I'd really rather not. It's much better for you if I don't. But if you're going to act like Rheigan, I won't hesitate."

"What's a Rheigan?" she asked, stalling for time and wondering how difficult it would be to get past the catlike woman and find her way home on her own.

"The Rheigans are currently the reigning sovereign power. They are supreme warriors, extremely intelligent, completely no-nonsense, and utterly grouchy and boorish—even the females. I expect much better manners in my patients," Xnam answered matter-of-factly. "Now lie down."

"You're not speaking my language," Kricket noted suspiciously, "yet I understand you perfectly."

"The language center of your brain has been stimulated with a program that will enable you to communicate efficiently in the standard languages we utilize," Xnam explained patiently, her frustration growing. The girl was turning out to be more stubborn than an Ulsan mule, and, given her diminutive size, hardly as docile as she would have assumed. "Lie down."

"What else has my brain been stimulated with?" Kricket asked in a cold, deadly tone that made the Redan physician pause and regard her cautiously.

She was tiny for a human female and esthetically very Delsheni. Her hair was slightly darker, hinting at her Rheigan ancestry, but not so much that anyone would suspect that her genetics ran along those lines. The hardness in her eyes belied the truth though. They were a lovely shade of deep, soft, bluish gray that many females would envy her for. But the wariness and the sharp, calculating intelligence behind them was pure Rheigan; it made Xnam shiver and the hairs along her skin rise.

She knew better, had seen the girl's genetic maps, knew she was only a quarter Rheigan blood, but the feeling of the girl's aura belied scientific fact.

"Infusions other than for basic communication purposes are illegal," Xnam stated pertly, giving Kricket and equally stern look in return. "We have only your best interests at heart, Kricket. Lie down…now."

Kricket regarded her calmly for exactly three seconds, not flinching, not moving, her piercing gray eyes seeming to bore into the doctor's soul, then slowly lowered herself onto the bed. As soon as her head rested back on the table, Xnam nodded sharply, as if approving, then turned and disappeared into the depths of the medical bay.

"You shouldn't cross her," William warned. "She's the prince's personal physician. What she sees and hears goes directly back to him."

"Prince?" Kricket countered waspishly. Her head hurt, she was sick to her stomach, and she was scared out of her mind. *"Seriously?"*

"The emperor's grandson," he supplied. "You've caught his notice, god help you."

"Why?" she asked cautiously, head turning and eyes regarding him curiously. "William, what's going on?"

"Not here," he cautiously and silently signed back, surprising her. "Everything is watched, recorded. Stay silent and play dumb. We'll see if we can get you home."

Home, Kricket thought bitterly. *As if home is so much better to return to.* Bits and pieces of the vision that had engulfed her earlier floated to the surface of her waking mind. The garden was dead; there was no going home.

CHAPTER FIVE

"I find the disparity between your report and Dr. Xnam's disturbing," Jaget said coolly. He was having a difficult time speaking civilly to the strange-looking man, and it showed in his tone.

The Professor shifted slightly in his chair, face neutral, trying to keep his rebellious heartbeat under control. He didn't entirely succeed. Small beads of perspiration formed on his brow, and his hands began to tremble slightly, as did the mad display of bluish-white hair jutting outward from his head. It wouldn't do at all to get caught—would ruin everything actually.

"The results are from your ship's own medical computers," he sputtered, as if daring the captain to deny the obvious.

"Which security scans reveal have been tampered with in a unique and disturbing manner," Jaget responded icily. "Strange that you thought to bring me the report yourself rather than allow the physician in charge of the girl to report her findings on her own."

"I only meant to assist," the Professor stammered, squirming visibly. "I've known the family for years. The girl is—"

"The girl is of both Rheigan and Delsheni royal ancestry, hardly a mongrel," Coltame supplied, tiring of the cat and mouse game the captain was playing. The Professor was guilty as sin of hiding the girl and her family. Everyone in the room knew it—even the Professor's son, who was all but cowering in the corner until he was called upon to speak. "In fact, her genetic chart is so meticulous, one could speculate it was artificially designed in a laboratory."

Curiously, at the prince's revelation, the boy sat up straighter, genuinely surprised and interested, but his father reeled dramatically as if struck. He then seemed to melt into his chair, his body slumping in defeat, yet his eyes zigzagged wildly back and forth as if calculating his next course of action, like a computer scanning for data after unexpectedly forced to reboot.

"How much were you aware of, Professor?" Ceya asked gently, playing the devil's advocate. Dealing with the legendary Professor DeSirpi had been one of the more unique experiences in her life, and she was quickly tiring of it. His behavior surpassed eccentricity. She doubted he was mad, but he played the part exceptionally well. In response, he jumped in his seat and swirled to face her, as if startled to suddenly find himself in a room with others.

"Professor, Ceya asked you a question," Jaget said coldly, not bothering to hide his frustration. "How much were you aware of?"

"Who knows?" the Professor offered oddly, gesturing wildly with his hands. "The universe is full of people—most of whom don't want to be bothered or discovered. I certainly can't be responsible for recognizing something that can't be seen behind closed doors."

It is all going to hell and very quickly, thought Professor DeSirpi. They had been so close; it had been nearly perfect. After years and years of waiting, it was finally all coming together and then that moron Malizore had gotten nervous and ruined everything.

"Perhaps we should call the mother in." Jaget interjected

CHAPTER FIVE

wearily.

"What could she possibly tell you?" the Professor blustered.

"The girl is of three purebred lines, meticulously spliced together," Jaget responded coldly. "In my experience that doesn't simply happen naturally."

"Everyone knows colonists keep to themselves," the Professor gibbered. "They're a very private sort of people. Waste of time and resources, if you ask me."

Coltame sat back in frustration but refused himself the luxury of losing his temper. It was too convenient that the universe's foremost expert in robotic warfare just happened to exile himself to the very colony that Hollin had hidden his family in. He had chosen to befriend the girl's mother, set up his household next door to her; he knew something.

"You are free to return to your quarters," Jaget pronounced coldly. "But do not leave them."

He was tired of the Professor's games. The strange man had worn out his welcome on his ship weeks before the girl's rescue, and his behavior since that time only cemented in his mind that DeSirpi was no ally to the Delsheni, possibly not even to the empire. That left only an allegiance to Malizore and the Roan. There was no doubt in his mind that the Roan would not have moved the core of their operations into the middle of nowhere simply because of increased pressure by imperial forces. Malizore would never give up that easily and, despite propaganda to the contrary, he had never been that far from gaining the upper edge. As Coltame had said, there was absolutely no reason for him to retreat into the backwater, except, perhaps, for the promise of Hollin's robot.

The Professor rose anxiously at his dismissal, flustered and agitatedly murmuring nonsense to himself. His eyes darted between each of the three officials questioning him, and his hands twisted nervously together. He began to speak, then closed his mouth, deciding against it. Abruptly his jittering behavior stopped. He bowed serenely and respectfully to each to them, as if he'd just risen from a casual luncheon or tea and would take his leave of them, then turned and strode airily from the room.

Jaget's sharp, cold eyes followed the man as he exited, but he refused to turn his head to watch as his sister did. Ceya was no fool. She wasn't a true empathic, as her father had been, but she was remarkably adept at studying the intricacies of human behavior and reading gestures that revealed what words alone couldn't. Turning his head toward her, he saw her gaze follow the old man. Then she exchanged a knowing look with her son before turning her head and smiling warmly at the boy shrinking into the shadows of room, alone and utterly forgotten by his father.

William wasn't surprised to be left without a backward glance. He'd never been one of his father's favorite people. He wasn't sure why he'd even been born, except perhaps to prove to the universe that his father was capable of having children. Once he'd made his entry into the world, however, he'd been just as forgotten as any of the thousands of other experiments his father had completed and shelved throughout the years.

Despite having what the school psychologists labeled as severe social anxieties and phobias, he was no fool. His father had been playing a dangerous game for years, and now everything was coming home to roost. Before today he had no idea that Kricket was a purebred, but he knew her mother was, so he wasn't entirely surprised. What lay before him was a choice. In a universe at war with itself, choices and sides were inevitable, but what he did now would not only decide his fate but that of his only friend as well.

He felt horrible for having dragged her into the mess they were in. He should never have returned to the surface after accepting a position on board the ship, but they had wanted information about the colony, a chance to see if anyone else wanted to be evacuated before they left, and he'd felt extremely guilty that he was about to leave without her.

Unfortunately people were executed daily for being on the wrong side. The Delsheni and the Rheigans were technically one ruling empire, but life was always more complicated than that.

CHAPTER FIVE

The two races combined their strengths and talents and got along well enough if they had to, but they also played their superpowers against one another just below the surface: the Rheigans firmly in power, the Delsheni thirsty to regain it. Caught in the middle were the rest of the human races. It was fairly obvious his father was playing more than one side. It would now be up to the son to prove where he stood.

Although he was not truly a coward, he was also no martyr to stupid causes. He was not willing to be offered up as a sacrificial lamb, which, there was no doubt, his father would do if he thought it necessary to save his own hide. In the end it came down to loyalty. He honestly didn't care whether he served the Delsheni or the Rheigans; there was only one person in the universe he genuinely cared enough about to choose for. Kricket had been his friend far too long, had stood up for him when no one else would, had been there when no one else cared. He would not ever, under any circumstances, betray her.

As all eyes at the conference table turned to regard him, he fought off his initial instinct to cringe. He took a deep breath, sat up a little straighter, and faced them with as much courage as he could muster, which wasn't much, given the gravity of what he was now expected to do.

"What do you need to know?" he asked.

***

Kricket padded softly in her bare feet across the medical bay inside the suite of rooms she was assigned to. She didn't know what had become of her shoes, but it didn't matter. She let her eyes wander lazily across the different control panels, stopping to examine the images of other patients, all the while sizing up the large man guarding the panel that she knew was the exit from the sick bay; at least she thought he was a man. At first glance, she had assumed he was human, but, on closer inspection, she wasn't so sure.

He was exceptionally tall and extremely muscular, and there

was no doubt that he was assigned to either keep others out or to keep her in. He had unusually pale skin and light blue, almost translucent eyes. His long, straight hair was paler than his skin and tied back at the nape.

He didn't wear the uniform that the others did. Instead a thin metal band wound around his neck, a vest loosely covered his thick chest and shoulders, and he wore an odd, Capri-like pants that exposed his calves and bare feet. He was at ease, and his eyes stared straight forward, ignoring her, but there was no doubt in her mind that he was on guard and knew exactly where she was at all times.

"What are you doing out of bed?" a young technician asked, entering the bay through a panel Kricket hadn't seen open yet. He was small and young, and she sensed her chance to escape might have just opened up.

"I'm not tired," she answered in a childlike voice, opening her large, gray eyes innocently wide, like a little girl. Occasionally, being ridiculously short came in handy. It worked; he put his data board down and approached authoritatively.

"You need to get back—"

He never finished. Faster than he could have anticipated, Kricket landed a swift kick to the left side of his head. She then curled her leg inward toward her stomach and then out again, striking him with a second kick to the sternum that sent him tumbling backward. She leaped over him and headed for the panel, banging her fist against a glowing light that had flashed when the tech entered. The panel opened, and she shot forward.

What she hadn't counted on was how fast the large guard at the other door could move. An instant later, his iron-like arms were around her, pinning her own arms to her sides. She growled in frustration, her feet lifting up off the floor and kicking him as she struggled, but the vise grip didn't budge. She saw Dr. Xnam and a few others come running from down the long, narrow hallway.

As the doctor approached, Kricket stopped struggling and went perfectly still, but her eyes continued to dart down one side

CHAPTER FIVE

of the hall and then the other. Predictably, the guard loosened his grip on her. An instant later she shrugged forcibly, loosening it further. Without thinking, her own hand attached at what she hoped were the pressure points of his hands and spun herself around and under him. Realizing she couldn't hope to ever control his arm, she changed tactics. She sidestepped and flipped him up and over her hip toward the approaching medical staff.

Without waiting to see if she'd been effective or not, she spun and leapt back toward the entrance to the sick bay, hoping to make it out the other panel now that it wasn't watched over. Her guard, however, was quicker than she anticipated. He succeeded in grabbing her ankle, tripping her, and sending her tumbling toward the floor.

"Don't hurt her!" Xnam shouted, even as Kricket began jabbing her free leg at the man in frantic kicks. As he pulled her closer, she was able to smash his nose and then his chin, causing the doctor to wince in sympathy. "Kricket, calm down," she ordered, watching as the guard subdued the girl's free leg and gradually wrapped himself around her in a human straightjacket.

"I want to go home," Kricket snarled, struggling against the solid restraint she found herself in. "You can't keep me here forever."

"Bring her back inside," Xnam responded, looking up and down the hallway to see who was watching. She groaned inwardly as she realized that a plethora of new rumors were sure to spread like wildfire through the large population on board. It hadn't been disclosed yet that she was Hollin's descendent, but Kricket was already a legend in her own right, and everyone, from patients to staff, were asking after her. "Nuzin, come with me and attend the Nubalah. Based on the blood, I think she's broken his nose."

Without preamble, Kricket felt herself being lifted as if she were no more than a paper doll and carried, face forward, back into her suite of rooms.

Once inside, the catlike doctor turned and faced her. "Kricket, you have two choices," she said in the scolding tone of a parent about to give a lecture. "You can either behave, or I can tranquilize you."

"I want to go home," Kricket repeated defiantly.

"You are not sufficiently recovered to take on a Latoni Nubalah like that," Xnam continued as if she hadn't heard her. "You're going to damage yourself, which will get the entire staff here in trouble. Do you really want that?"

"I honestly don't give a damn," she answered rudely in return. "I was captured and brought here against my will. I want to go home."

"You were not captured," Xnam corrected firmly. "You were brought here for medical treatment, of which you are doing a very good job of undoing."

"Fine," she spat back, eyes angry and rebellious. "I feel much better now. Thank you for all your efforts. May I please go home now?"

Xnam swallowed the feline growl that rose in her throat, but there was no mistaking the irritation in her catlike eyes. "It's not that simple," she replied flatly, turning away and then turning back. "Do you understand what a spaceship is?" she asked. When the girl nodded, she added, "And do you understand what happens to humans when they open the wrong panel? They get sucked out into space and explode very quickly."

"I'm told it's supposedly painless," she responded blandly, nonplussed.

"Let her go," Xnam ordered flatly, eyes not leaving the girl. When the guard complied and stepped away to receive the treatment of the technician, she continued in a soft, but firm tone. "Has William explained why you're here?"

Kricket shook her head no in answer. He might have told her, but until the last half hour or so, she'd been too drugged to notice, let alone remember. The doctor turned and picked up what Kricket assumed was some kind of diagnostic tool and ran it over her body several times. Apparently not liking the results, she repeated the procedure, then sternly lifted her eyes back up.

"You've healed very quickly for a human," she pronounced.

CHAPTER FIVE

"Other than some minor swelling and bruising, I can see very little trace of the damage Malizore did to you...Although the Nubalah seems to have inflicted a few new sprains," she added, giving the guard a look that clearly showed she was not pleased.

Kricket shrugged her shoulders nonchalantly. "I'm a quick healer," she answered simply. It was true. She'd always been able to rapidly recover from injuries, and in her martial arts training since the invaders had come, there'd been many of them.

Xnam regarded her coolly for several long seconds before asking, "Do you understand why you're here?"

"Obviously I don't," she responded pertly.

"You're here," the physician began in a firm, controlled voice, "because you succeeded in doing what no one has been able to do for a very long time. You wounded, perhaps mortally, the pirate and self-proclaimed emperor of the Roan—the people who are currently occupying your planet. Although most will cheer your actions and laud you a heroine, many will not. As we speak, Malizore's agents are trying to find you so that they can make a very public example of you with a prolonged and painful execution. If you are returned home, those same agents will not only find you, they will find your family, your friends, your neighbors—anyone who has ever been associated with you. And all of them will be rounded up, publicly tortured, and then executed as an example to others who might think of taking similar actions as yours."

Kricket swallowed hard as the physician's words sank in and brought back memories of the vision that had sent her fighting to get out of bed and looking for the exit. He was coming for her, and she had to be ready, but what that meant baffled her. All she knew was that he was looking for her. She couldn't let him find her, just as she couldn't let the Professor...*What? What can't I let him do?* She asked silently. The memory of it was thickly hidden behind the fog of her dreams and refused to be pieced together.

"Is he okay?" she asked simply, jutting her chin in the

direction of the guard.

Xnam blinked hard, caught off guard by the girl's sudden shift in attitude. "He's a Nubalah, a Latoni warrior." She answered as if that in itself should make sense. "They don't break easily."

Kricket nodded as if she understood, but she honestly didn't. It was all strange and bizarre and extremely frightening. The vision she'd had was only clear about two things: the garden was dead and she was in grave danger. The visions, though always unwanted, were never wrong. Unfortunately she still had to figure out what that danger was. This would not be simple, as the visions were often not clear based just on the images she was given.

"He's been assigned to protect you." Xnam continued, "In his simple understanding, your life has been placed in his protection. If you die, he's failed, and the dishonor of that failure will either force him to commit suicide or his brother warriors will kill him instead. He's not your jailor, Kricket; he's your guardian."

At the physician's use of the word guardian, Kricket's head snapped up. The guardian had been mentioned several times in her vision, but she wasn't sure what that meant. *It was time for the guardian* —that was the message. But who that was and how she was supposed to facilitate it, she didn't know. That was the problem with her visions: they took control over her, but she rarely remembered everything they showed her. They were often vague and her understanding of them easy to misinterpret.

Xnam's eyes narrowed as the girl's eyes suddenly sharpened. She doubted it had been her explanation of the guard that alerted Kricket; it had to be something associated with it. Mentally replaying her words, she found the only word that might have had a double meaning. *So*, she thought to herself, *the girl might not be so ignorant of her ancestry after all.*

***

"She is aboard the *Nadir*." Maerwynn reported. "But she

CHAPTER FIVE

can't hide forever behind Jaget's skirts," she added hastily.

"I have every confidence in you," Malizore responded absently from his command chair. A richly embroidered tapestry had been draped over it, hiding the fact that he was propped up with pillows and blankets, but it was obvious that he was still in pain. "Because you know what will happen to you if you fail to retrieve her," he finished with a deadly calmness.

Maerwynn sucked in her breath but managed to pull a seductive smile out of it. Malizore rarely threatened her, but, then again, she'd never truly given him a reason to. She was his most competent general, as well as his lover, and she had leapt to the forefront of the hunt to discover the girl's identity and avenge her ruler's brutal mauling. Unfortunately things hadn't been as easy as she had assumed they would be. How could they be with a Federation battleship orbiting the planet's surface?

"I will assign Vat and Sumner to ferret her out," she stated, thinking it might be best to shift the attention, and the blame, elsewhere. She was far better suited to standing behind the throne and reminding her lord that she was ever his, rather than in front of it groveling in defeat.

"And the Professor?" Malizore snarled. No one failed him without consequences, ever, but Maerwynn was not just anyone. She had proven herself time and again to him, her loyalty unquestionable, and he needed her now more than ever.

He had been essentially castrated by the little bitch and her penknife. How, he couldn't fathom, but the pain of its repair had been excruciating, and none of his physicians could assure him that he'd ever function again as a male without assistance. Children he had enough of, but there were many worlds in which he operated where a man's virility was everything. He needed Maerwynn to continue as his lover, to swear to the universe he was still a man...So for now he allowed her uncharacteristic failure slide.

"He is also aboard the *Nadir*," she answered, but this time she smiled when she delivered the news. "But he has made contact."

"And his explanation for his behavior?" he demanded.

"That he must show many faces to the universe. But he swears his undying allegiance, asks you to remember his years of service, and begs you to wait just a little longer—"

"I have been waiting more than two decades!" he roared, nearly rising from his dais, but deciding against it as the pain of the movement restricted him.

"He assures you that he is very close," she added in a gentle, consoling tone. "He—"

"He's an idiot…you're all idiots…I'm surrounded by idiots," He snarled. "Worthless fools…all of you."

Maerwynn bowed low, accepting her lord's accusations; she understood. DeSirpi had been promising the secret of the Sentinel Guardian for years. Only the staggered delivery of a few precious notes and schematics had kept Malizore's patience intact, but now he was wounded, and shamed, and tired of empty promises.

"Tell him that he must either prove his allegiance or be destroyed," he growled mercilessly, one eye narrowing and breath deepening, "Tell him to bring me the girl."

CHAPTER SIX

"The girl must be secured," Rastmus said firmly, his eyes hard and commanding, penetrating through the viewing screen on the wall which projected his image. "Her rapid rise to fame is too enormous to allow her to remain in Delsheni hands," he added. *Hollin's granddaughter*, he mused silently to himself. *Who in the universe could have ever anticipated that?* "The Professor has proven duplicitous before. Do not allow him access to her until her transport back to Syphlein can be arranged."

"I don't believe sending her immediately back to Syphlein is the wisest course," Coltame responded cautiously, well aware that his father would not take kindly to being contradicted. In Rheigan society, the patriarch's will was law, always—especially among the royals.

His father was about as high in the imperial hierarchy as you could get. He was not only a biological son of the emperor, he was a recognized son. In a universe where humanity was struggling to bring itself back from the brink of extinction, formal recognition meant everything. Perfect bloodlines could no longer be assured now that laboratory breeding was out of favor; it was up to the parent to decide through which offspring the line would continue. The general consensus was that biological children happened, but birth order and parentage were not necessarily the keys to succession—especially in regard to the imperial heirs.

Just as the younger man predicted, Rastmus tensed at his son's remark, anger flashing in his stern eyes and ready to attack unless a suitable explanation for the defiance was offered. Without waiting, Coltame launched into his explanation.

"She's very young, and there's very little evidence she understands what's happening to her," he continued. "She has no reason to trust us over the Professor, whom she's known her entire life. To take her away from her family will be hard enough on her, but to leave her fate to a society that she doesn't understand and isn't capable of navigating could prove disastrous. It might embitter her against the empire. She might grow to consider us the source of her strife rather than the protector against her enemies, to which she should throw her allegiance and her loyalties. It might give our adversaries ground to persuade her to their causes; we might lose her and whatever information she may have inherited."

"What are you suggesting?" his father asked, eyes narrowing and boring into him through the screen.

"She's young and, one could assume, there might be another way to secure her loyalties," Coltame offered as indifferently as he could manage. It was hard enough to go up against his father over an issue that he cared nothing about, but this was personal. He didn't believe it was a coincidence that the girl had been delivered into his life within hours of being given a vision of her. She was sent to him by the gods themselves; he was sure of it. He wanted to be her protector and felt a duty to the deities who had arranged it, but wanting something made negotiating for it a thousand times more difficult.

"Such as…" his father prompted when a short silence fell between them. He didn't tolerate contrary opinions well, especially from his offspring, but there was a merit to his

CHAPTER SIX

argument that he had already considered, so he would hear the boy out.

"Such as aligning her in a quick first union with someone loyal who could win her confidence," Coltame suggested, doing his best to keep his voice level and indifferent despite his racing heart. "Someone who could keep her safe from Malizore and the prying eyes of the court, who could educate her about our society and what is expected of her, make her feel safe, encourage her to trust her family secrets..."

"And the male counterpart to the alliance you have in mind?" Rastmus asked drolly; he wasn't fooled a bit. His son had learned a great deal in his years at court, but he was no match for a father who had dedicated his entire life to it. He had already secretly been informed by the boy's mother of the events surrounding the girl, including Coltame's surprising fascination with her and what that enthrallment had uncovered.

"Me," he said coolly, his heart pounding rebelliously in his chest. He had no idea what his father's response would be. The idea was ludicrous. She was Hollin's offspring. Any alliance between the progeny of an unknown Delsheni royal and a known Rheigan traitor would be considered highly unacceptable—unless the empire could profit from it.

"There are more favorable choices under development for your next alliance," Rastmus responded icily, resisting the urge to smile. He'd been right, as usual: the boy had nominated himself.

"Choices more advantageous than the location of Hollin's Sentinel Guardian?" Coltame countered. "More advantageous than thwarting Malizore and perhaps ending once and for all the threat of the Trogoul?"

"If the girl is ignorant of the information needed, then any union with her is a wasted alliance," his father replied dismissively, as if the matter were unworthy to waste valuable time considering.

"Not a one-year, informal bonding," he argued, ready with a prepared defense. "If it shows promise, then it could be renewed.

If not—"

"Any offspring produced would not be suitable," his fathered parried, wondering how far the boy would take his arguments. He'd only met the girl a few days before. His own mother was baffled by the apparent infatuation. Then again, hadn't he perplexed his own father with his infatuation with Ceya? From the instant he'd first laid eyes on her in the halls of the Delsheni Academy, he'd known he wanted her—but those were musings for a different time. "She's too young to breed," he continued dismissively. "She won't come of age for at least another year, possibly two. Whatever branch of family claims her would never agree to pairing her until she matures."

"They would if she were already compromised," Coltame offered carefully, although ashamed to stoop so low as to insinuate it. Social laws were incredibly strict. If science couldn't guarantee the genes of the next generation, then the laws mandating pairings would have to be; their punishment was harsh on young offenders. He knew what he was suggesting unfairly maligned her, but there was no time to construct other, more respectable arguments.

Rastmus's eyebrows raised slightly, despite himself. "Has she been?"

Coltame swallowed hard, remembering William's testimony about the world in which they had grown to adulthood. "The moral code of the culture in which she's been reared is questionable at best," he began, noticing his father's sudden intense interest. "We have reliable testimony that, from an unsuitably young age, she has had more than one unsupervised encounter with a male suitor," he presented uneasily, knowing even as he did so that he might be unjustifiably slandering her. "It's a safe assumption."

He paused and let his words sink through his father's thoughts, the deepening frown on his forehead indicating he was sifting through the possible ramifications. Premarital affairs were not tolerated, and young adults were closely monitored and chaperoned. Engaging in any form of inappropriate contact was

CHAPTER SIX

a serious breach of the moral code and, in many cases, punishable by law. He doubted any tribunal assigned to hear accusations of it would ever seriously censure her—she couldn't be held responsible for the society in which she was brought up—but the court of public opinion would slaughter her. The girl was an instant celebrity, already touted on the news and information systems as a heroine of extraordinary bravery. An instant icon that the propaganda houses desperately needed. Heroes and heroines were expected to be upstanding citizens, examples beyond reproach. If the empire planned to use her at all in their literature, which he was sure they would, she would also have to have an outstanding moral character to complement her bravery; that wouldn't happen if she'd been compromised.

"You have evidence of this...*behavior?*" Rastmus inquired icily. Hollin had been a master of public policy, his ability to catapult his name and image into legendary stardom nearly as impressive as his abilities as a heroic soldier; his granddaughter would be expected to continue that. The propaganda wheels had already begun spinning, but if the girl turned out to be an unprincipled yokel instead of a goddess-like heroine from Annon, there were many prominent people, politicians and royals both, who would suffer the embarrassment of supporting her hasty rise to fame in her ancestor's shadow.

Coltame paused and considered his words. They already knew the girl wasn't compromised in the way he insinuated, but William had testified that she could be a flirt and that her society didn't forbid interactions between unmarried adolescents. "The society in which the colony is based is reminiscent of the Nolaje," he offered, hoping his father would draw his own conclusions. The Nolaje were a society of human mongrels that, while not exactly vagrants, weren't precisely known for their propriety. Their home world was the place all young men gravitated to at one time or another, particularly if they were in search of female company that wouldn't require marriage contracts in return for a little fun.

"Evidence," his father repeated frigidly, reluctant to make any decision based on speculation.

Coltame paused, hesitant to disparage the girl any further, but, by the same token, unwilling to lose this particular argument with his father. "She has been seen publicly by at least one imperial civilian engaging in...questionable activities involving skin-to-skin contact," he offered judiciously, watching carefully as his father absorbed the new information he'd presented.

He was exaggerating, but William had admitted that he knew she'd allowed her suitors to kiss her, which Coltame intended to use to his full advantage if he needed to. Kissing, while still practiced by many behind closed doors, had been practically phased out of the germophobic society humans had evolved into. The mouth was the dirtiest part of the human body—a human bite was extremely infectious. To a society obsessed about their genetics and lack of viruses and bacteria, the idea of coming into contact with it was repugnant. *People still do it*, he mused silently. *But you'll never find anyone who'll admit to it- especially since the definition of the consummation of marriage hasbeen broadened to a simple "transfer of bodily fluids." By that description, even the coldest of arranged marriages can be sanctioned by a simple kiss on the hand.*

"A one-year alliance could provide a safe explanation for any...obvious indiscretions of her cross-cultural experience," Coltame offered. "In the year that follows, I can earn her trust, discover her secrets." *And*, he added silently, *I can buy time against whatever contract you're negotiating for me, while ferreting out why the gods I thought I didn't believe in sent her into my care.*

"And at the end of that one- year term, you are both free to renegotiate more formal agreements, which would, by law, take precedence over any negotiated contracts with the Duke of Horshell's daughter," Rastmus added dryly. "Your willingness to sacrifice yourself in service to your empire is commendable," he added, the sarcasm evident.

He knew very well his son was aware of, and ready to argue against, the alliance currently under negotiation, but it surprised

CHAPTER SIX

him that he was willing to jump into a hasty marriage with a total stranger to avoid it. The duke's daughter, had she been born male, would have had a stronger claim to the Rheigan throne than Coltame had. It was a far better match, even if the two partners were unwilling. His son would have no choice; none of them did. He was a recognized grandson of the emperor and would marry who he was told to.

He sympathized with the boy though. He knew all too well what it was like to be trapped with a shrew of a wife when the spouse you wanted was forbidden to you because of conflicting birthrights. He doubted Coltame had much in the way of feelings for the girl past simple curiosity or perhaps an obsession with her ancestry. It was more likely that his son was less than enthusiastic about the other match. Perhaps a year would give him time to come to terms with the inevitable. It was an indulgence he would not have shown any of his other children, but Coltame was his only son—and he was Ceya's son. Besides, he reasoned to himself, it isn't entirely unsuitable. Hollin's legend had reached mythical proportions during his absence, and the girl's genome chart read better than the current emperor's. If she hadn't been three quarters Delsheni, he might have considered her a stronger candidate for his son, but his future grandchildren needed more Rheigan blood if Coltame was to secure his place as heir to the empire. Then again, there were many who had wanted Hollin instead of his own father, and they were sure to raise their heads again now that his heir had re-emerged.

Also to be considered was the problem of Hollin's granddaughter emerging out of nowhere and taking down Malizore in her first encounter. Hollin had been branded a traitor by the emperor, but few actually considered him so. His legend was sure to revive with a living heir to the legacy. A child was rarely legally condemned to the same fate as his ancestors, but society was fickle. It would be difficult for the emperor to publicly acknowledge the fame of the girl without acknowledging the line from which she was descended. A short, one-year contract with his son, however, might solve that problem nicely. Coltame was still considered too far removed from the immediate line of succession to be a serious contender for the throne, a fact Rastmus fought desperately to change, but he was still the emperor's grandson. By acknowledging an informal union between him and the girl, her status as a worthy member of society was assured without the emperor ever having to formally acknowledge her bloodline.

"Very well," he agreed, stunning his son. "I shall sign off on a one year bonding. But after that you will swear to end it and return home to do your duty to this family and the empire."

Coltame resisted the urge to drop his jaw in surprise. He had expected more resistance, which instantly made him wonder what advantage the match had inadvertently produced. The gods had sent her to him, he was sure of it, and, as if proving so, once again divine intervention seemed to reveal itself in his father's unexpected approval.

"Thank you, Father," he replied formally, with a slight bow. "I won't fail you," he added dutifully, just as he had thousands of times since he was a child.

"See that you don't," his father replied coldly, then ended his transmission.

***

"Goman..." the Emperor Zoujin summoned, his deep, growling voice weak and frail, even to his own ears. He didn't feel weak: his mind raced, sharp as ever, and his dark black eyes were free of cataracts and missed nothing. Yet his body failed him. His limbs were twisted and grotesque, his face sunken beneath the paper-thin skin clinging to his skull.

"Your Eminence..." the old sage answered, shuffling forward and struggling to kneel to the marble floor and bow low on ancient limbs that had to be as stiff and painful as the emperor's own.

Goman was the emperor's senior by a full decade. He was a

CHAPTER SIX

tiny man, quiet and meek. He was, and always had been, his lord's most trusted vizier. Gifted since birth with the powers of second Sight, he had the ability to stare into the souls of those who approached the absolute ruler of several dozen worlds and see the truths and conniving behind their words—an invaluable asset.

"Rise," Zoujin commanded, although the deep rumble was barely more than a hoarse whisper.

Goman didn't appear to struggle, but he was slow to pull his body upward. Any other man, aged or not, would have been executed immediately for such disrespect, but Goman was no ordinary member of the court. The emperor understood it was only the force of his indomitable spirit that moved his ancient limbs. His aged and faded blue eyes were the last to elevate into place, leveling into a lock on his sovereign that no other living being would dare.

"We have heard the walls whispering," Zoujin hissed. Just because he was old didn't mean he couldn't still hear everything around him. There were far too many who assumed the frailty of his body extended to his mind as well; they were wrong.

"Yes, Your Grace," Goman answered, head bowing as low as he dared without the risk of tumbling over, his arms leaning heavily on the staff he used to remain upright.

"A name has been mentioned that we have not heard for many years," Zoujin hissed. He wasn't sure what angered him more: that Hollin's hiding place had finally been publicly uncovered or that no one had bothered to bring the news to him first.

"Yes, Your Majesty."

"Many years ago," Zoujin began, then paused and closed his eyes, the memory still painful, even after all the decades that had passed. "We had you scribe for us," he finished, black eyes opening and boring coldly into his servant.

"I remember, My Lord," Goman answered, bowing again in acknowledgement.

"This girl…this hellion who has maimed our illegitimate

upstart and excited the populace: she is *Meera's* daughter?" he asked, referring to Hollin's mistress who had had the audacity to declare herself the wife of his brother's heart.

"Descendent, My Lord. But, in the eyes of the gods, that is considered one and the same," he added gently, hiding his amusement. He knew it would not be long before the emperor heard the rumors. What he wasn't sure of, however, was his reaction. He might simply damn the girl outright for her heritage, holding her responsible for the provocations of her ancestors, but, then again, his sovereign's curiosity just might get the better of him.

"You must go to her," Zoujin decreed, resisting the urge to smile wickedly at the horror forming in Goman's eyes. Travel, for both of them, was nearly impossible now. A journey to the edge of the known universe, even in the best accommodations, would be living torture. "Only you know if she is the one you saw. Only you can interpret your own vision and inform us of the wisest course of our next action."

Goman continued to stare at his lord, as if waiting for the jest to end, but the old monarch simply gazed back at him. Eventually he bowed deeply, accepting the first task in decades that was just as likely to kill him as please his liege.

"You may go," the emperor decreed.

***

Coltame raised an eyebrow at the quickness by which his summons was answered, but otherwise showed no outward emotion as William entered his office, dropped to his knees, and bowed low in a show of unworthiness.

"I'm not the emperor," he stated blandly, rolling his eyes heavenward at the inappropriateness of the boy's actions. "Nor am I my father who might prematurely enjoy such supplication in his loyal followers. A simple nod or slight bow in recognition of my rank is all that is required."

"I wasn't sure," William answered nervously, rising to his

CHAPTER SIX

feet and fidgeting anxiously. He might not require it, but the prince still had the power of life or death over him; better safe than sorry. "I wasn't brought up in mainstream society, and one of the techs said—"

"One of the techs said what?" Coltame snapped. He was getting tired of the gossip that had surrounded him since his last visit to his grandfather's palace.

"That...you're in favor..." William stammered fretfully. "That you're being...considered."

"I assure you there are far more aggressive candidates who seek the throne with far more zeal than I," he responded drolly.

His grandfather, the emperor, was dying. No one would deny that. He was an ancient man who had lived far beyond his years and who only now survived through the shear tenaciousness of his spirit. In his heyday, Emperor Zoujin had been a formidable presence, and that legacy, more than anything else, kept the swarm of hopeful successors at bay long enough for him to expire of natural causes.

He was not that concerned. His father—although the son of a later wife and not the grand empress—was among the top favored for succession, but not him. Coltame was his father's only biological son and, as such, was thrust into the limelight along with him. But he seriously doubted, should his father be chosen as heir, he would succeed to the throne after him. For one thing, there were several overly aggressive cousins who wanted that distinction far more than he did, and, for another, both his mother and his paternal grandmother had been Delsheni. Although he looked the part of a Rheigan prince, his blood and his soul were simply not Rheigan enough.

His father was still hoping to remedy that one glaringly obvious defect by aligning him with a flawlessly purebred Rheigan female with which to produce an heir. If Coltame could generate a son with a decent enough pedigree, and if Rastmus could manage to live as long as his father had, then perhaps those in power could overlook the obvious; but he doubted that would happen. He wasn't interested in reproducing for the benefit of the empire. He had several illegitimate children, male and female, with his mistresses, which proved his abilities. Nothing could have tempted him to procreate with the last wife they'd forced upon him, and he seriously doubted the newest candidate would interest him in the production an heir either.

"I require your cooperation," Coltame stated, shifting his thoughts and changing the subject in the same breath.

William nodded; he'd been expecting that. Once you chose a side, you were asked to do things to prove your allegiance. He wasn't his father; he wasn't able to play all sides at once. He was only himself. He expected he would be assigned to report on his father's activities. He was the closest to him and the least suspected to betray him, but that's not what followed.

"I need you to clarify matters relating to the interpersonal rituals of your peer group on the planet below," the prince began. "Specifically, what the female population requires in terms of building intimacy."

William blanched and almost immediately began to sweat profusely. He was the last person in the universe to explain the social customs of his previous peer group. He'd been a pariah. Worse than a pariah: he'd been tortured by them. "I'm not...I'm not..." he stammered, his eyes betraying his utter panic.

"I'm not asking for a step-by-step tutorial," Coltame replied dryly. He was already aware that the boy might not profess enough interest in the female population to bother learning how to seduce them. "I need to know the differences between our mainstream culture and theirs, or, if you don't know them, the basic sentiments or actions that would be considered endearing by females on the world below us. Actions your friend might appreciate, as well as those that would repel her."

When the boy continued to stare at him, he elaborated. "I need to know how to win Kricket's trust—that is her name, is it not? You were reared together. You understand her, understand her preferences— the actions or gestures that might entice her or inhibit progress toward intimacy?"

"Kirsten," William managed, although completely stunned to

CHAPTER SIX

his core. He couldn't fathom why the prince would need to know how to flatter her. "Her name, I mean...It's Kirsten. But she hates it, I mean seriously hates it, so everyone calls her Kricket...with a K. I mean cricket is normally spelled with a C, but her real name begins with a K, so in Kindergarten she decided to spell it with a K. She's always had a lot of energy and would hop around and was constantly talking about everything and nothing at the same time, which her brother said was like chirping...so cricket, but Kricket...with a K, I mean."

Coltame stared back at the boy blandly, suddenly aware the interview might not be as short as he'd anticipated. "Kricket...with a K," He repeated. "I will strive to remember that. Now tell me, what will entice her to trust me?"

"Trust?" William squeaked. Kricket didn't exactly trust anyone, not since her brothers disappeared anyway. She'd had too many strange things happen. "Trust..." he repeated, searching frantically for something to tell the young prince. "Um...Don't ever lie to her," he offered lamely. "She knows...I mean, she always knows when she's lied to."

This caught Coltame's interest, and he didn't bother to conceal his curiosity. "Explain," He demanded cautiously, leaning backward in his chair.

"Well, I don't know for sure, I mean...well...she's...she...she just knows...things."

"Does she have the Sight?" Coltame asked plainly, and noted instantly how the boy paled.

William felt as if he might faint at any moment. If Kricket had the Sight...That made so much more sense. Suddenly things he'd never considered before began falling into place with a rapidity that threatened to overwhelm him. "It..." he began, then swallowed hard, willing himself not to fall over with an unwanted realization that had hit him like a ton of bricks. What he said next could, possibly, depending on the view of the person he admitted it to, get him into a lot of trouble if he was wrong. "I never considered...I mean, I assumed...I always thought she was local, or at least half, you know...but...it...it would make sense…Your Highness."

Coltame closed his eyes and willed himself to remain calm. It made far more sense than the boy could ever possibly know.

CHAPTER SEVEN

Kricket sighed heavily, bored to tears and agitated with her confinement. She wanted something to do besides stare at her so-called guardian. If he was aware of the scrutiny, he didn't show it. He simply stared straight ahead, back to the door panel, arms crossed. In frustration, she lay back down on the medical bed and stared at the ceiling.

Did her mother even know what had happened to her? They had had their differences, especially in the past year since her brothers had disappeared, but she loved her and worried at the anguish her own disappearance would cause. No one captured by the invaders ever returned, but, in her case, she wasn't really captured; she just couldn't go back. Would anyone know the difference though?

Restless, she turned her body to one side, then the other, then onto her back. The lights had been dimmed to reflect the sleeping hours, but that was of very little help. The vision had warned her that she was in danger but, as usual, failed to explain itself or tell her where to look or what to be cautious of. She didn't know where she was or what would become of her, and she was frankly too frightened to ask. Sitting up again, she wrapped her arms around her legs, pressing her chin against her knees. It would be a lot more useful to know what it was she was trying to watch out for.

Before she could consider the idea too much longer, the door to the chamber outside her room swished open, and Professor DeSirpi strode through. He looked one way down the long room, then turned his head toward her and nodded, as if congratulating himself on finding her exactly where she was supposed to be.

"Good. You're awake," he said without preamble. "Come along now, off the table. Time to go."

"Go where?" she asked, surprised yet hopeful at the same time.

"Home," he answered, as if amazed she hadn't thought of it for herself. "You've healed. You're well. Your mother wants you. Time to go. They're very busy here, and you've taken up enough of their valuable time, yes, you have."

"But Dr. Xnam said I couldn't—"

"What's this?" he blustered. "What's this? What would she know of human matters, eh? Not even human, just a damn Redan—no sense of human matters, none. They raise their young as a collective…just pop them out two or three at a time and go on their merry way, assuming the rest of the tribe will raise them. Humans don't operate that way, no, they don't. We have our mothers and our mothers care for us. They want us back when we've gone missing, so off you go now…"

As he spoke, he gently but firmly pulled her from the table and began to nudge her in a staccato rhythm of taps toward the exit. As she made her way toward the large panel, she watched the Latoni warrior carefully, sure he would protest, but for some strange reason he didn't. Instead he just stepped aside and brought up the rear as they entered into a brightly lit hallway.

Few people were about and, those who were, passed her with little notice. Occasionally someone would look her up or down, taking in the strangeness of her garments and bare feet, but no one ever stopped them to investigate what they were up to. It

CHAPTER SEVEN

completely and totally baffled her. After struggling to gain her own freedom only hours before, was it simply just a matter of walking out the door with the right person?

"Kricket!" William squealed, stunned to see her as he rounded the corner. He'd spent the last few hours being grilled over and over on the intricacies of the traditions of his adopted planet. It had taken far longer than he'd anticipated, and he was only now on his way to see her before heading back to his quarters. "What are you doing out of bed?"

"She's healed," the Professor responded for her. "Her mother wants her back; it's time to go. Now say good night, and be off with you," he added in the agitation of an adult who was abruptly ending a playdate for reasons the children wouldn't understand.

"Dr. Xnam signed you out?" William asked cautiously. Something wasn't right. Not only was it incredibly odd that his father would take the initiative to bring Kricket home personally, William knew damn well that she couldn't go back. Malizore's forces were sure to find her if she returned, and there was no way those in charge would simply send her packing to face something like that alone.

"Are you questioning me, boy?" the Professor asked challengingly, all befuddlement aside, stepping toward his son as if to strike him.

The action was too reminiscent of his life at home, and William backed up automatically out of habit. His heart began to thud in his chest as he looked from his father, to Kricket, to the Nubalah assigned to protect her. The prince had said nothing about Kricket being released. In fact, he'd asked William to talk with her, to explain that she had to stay, that they were tracking down her family. There had been nothing said about her going back to her mother.

"Good night, Kricket," he said cautiously, exhaling the breath he'd been holding when his father nodded curtly and turned his back to him.

"Come along, girl. We'll miss our ride home," the Professor

called as he began to stride purposefully away.

Kricket paused briefly, giving William a cautious look, which he returned. "What?" She signed silently as the guard began to nudge her forward in the direction of her friend's father.

"Don't go," William signed with his fingers, surprising her.

Turning her head backward as the guard pushed her forward, she nodded quickly that she'd heard him, but she didn't understand. The Professor was William's father. He was odd and eccentric, but he'd known her all her life. *Why shouldn't I go with him?* she wondered, stomach sinking as they rounded the bend in the hall.

William took a few uneasy paces back and forth wondering what he should do. He didn't know how his father was planning on getting Kricket off the ship, but he doubted it was by traditional means. A shuttle or escape pod would be too easy to reel back in; that left a transport beam. He didn't have any kind of authority to directly access the bridge to alert them. He didn't even have permission to contact anyone who could notify them. If he ran back to the prince's quarters, providing they'd even let him up there without a summons, his father might have enough time to reach his scheduled rendezvous coordinates, and then he and Kricket would both be gone. Swallowing hard, he did the only thing he could think of: he hit the panic button on the side of his communicator.

***

"Sir?" one of the bridge technicians questioned in a frustrated tone.

"What is it?" Lieutenant Commander Gage asked, diverting his attention from the readouts on the captain's chair. He wasn't the true captain of the ship, like his father was, but every few months he rotated with several of the other junior commanders during the graveyard shift. They were rarely ever in charge of more than maintenance scans and the occasional repair shift after a battle, but it was good experience.

CHAPTER SEVEN

"One of the programming techs keeps setting off his panic device," the tech answered. "At first I thought it was a malfunction, but he keeps reactivating the beacon."

"What's his location?" Gage asked, frowning and coming to stand next to the tech.

"Deck twelve," he responded dryly.

"He's setting it off from inside the ship?" Gage asked in confusion. "Is this some kind of prank you guys play on each other?"

"No sir," the tech replied, his frustration evident as the panic signal was activated again. "Setting off those kinds of distress signals carry the same penalties as setting off any of the ship's alarms unnecessarily."

"Then find out what he wants," he suggested blandly, crossing his arms and giving the boy a good-natured look that suggested he was curious to know.

"Yes sir," the tech answered, then added, "P83451, please verbally confirm code twenty-seven distress."

"This is William DeSirpi..." William's whispered voice crackled through the line. "Um, programmer 83451. My father is Professor Piero DeSirpi. He has Kricket Holland, and I think he's getting ready to transport her off the ship. Someone needs to make sure the ship's shields don't have a bubble in them that he can get her out through."

"Is this some sort of joke?" Gage asked the technician, but the young man only stared back at him and shrugged. "Who the hell is Kricket Holland?"

"I think he means the girl," a female technician answered from across the darkened bridge. "The one they're talking about—the one who stabbed Malizore. She's supposedly sealed up in medical. There's also a high level security watch on the Professor, sir," she added.

"Full scan of all shields and all shield systems," Gage ordered, just to be cautious. "Bring reinforcement shielding up slowly so we don't set off alarms and wake the day crew. Scramble any signal probes that might bounce our way.

Someone get medical on the horn and find out if the girl is missing. If she is, someone get her bio signal loaded, and let's get a position on her."

"P83451, we're investigating now. Please do not reactivate your emergency signal," the tech advised.

"Thank god." William's relieved voice filtered through. "He's taking her straight to Malizore. You can't let him do that; he'll kill her."

That got their attention. Gage's eyebrows rose, and the other techs popped their heads up from their consoles to look at one another.

"Sir?" queried the female tech who had spoken before. She then continued when Gage looked in her direction. "Medical confirms that the girl is missing. They're uploading her signal now and are strongly urging you to separate her from the Professor and inform the Rheigan ambassador immediately."

"Get a fix on her, and do an inner transport back to the med bay," Gage ordered.

"The signal won't lock," another tech announced in confusion. "It's telling me it's locking, but it's not…All that transports is air. It's the same for both her and the Professor. It won't execute."

"He's probably reprogrammed the main console down in engineering in anticipation of getting caught," William's voice answered.

"Who left the goddamned channel open?" Gage sputtered in surprise, then rolled his eyes in frustration as the first technician sheepishly tapped a button to close it. "Open it back up!" he admonished in frustration. "DeSirpi's son already heard everything we've said. My god, you guys are greener than first-year cadets."

As the tech obliged, he continued, "All right, William, you have my attention. What are your suggestions?"

"Um," William's voice answered uncertainly, "it's not an easy thing to reprogram. You need specific exceptions, and then you can only really mute it. Try locking onto me, and see if it's

CHAPTER SEVEN

just their signatures you can't hold. If you can transport me to the bridge, then you can send me back to her. If I can get a good hold on her, you can use me to get a stronger signal lock."

As all eyes on the bridge turned to Gage, he shrugged, then nodded. "All right, let's try it. Bring him here." Then, as William's form materialized next to the main doors, Gage continued his instruction. "Now put him in proximity to the girl, but not where the Professor will realize what we're about to try. In the meantime, figure out what program is interfering with our equipment and run a full scan for holes in our shielding." Turning to William, he added brusquely, "You have exactly one minute to tackle that girl and transport back here before I call a general alert and put the shields up to maximum."

***

Kricket slowed her progress as the Professor led them through a side door and down a long, narrow passageway. This was obviously not an area for civilians. It was really no more than a service access—an open, metal catwalk clinging to the wall. The lighting was dim and the rumble of machinery loud in her ears. Eventually she came to a complete stop, staring at the complex machinery, blinking panels, and maze of connecting walkways, but the guard behind her pushed her forward.

The Professor wasn't lying to her. She always knew if people lied or if they were trying to deceive her; which was one of the main reasons she hadn't been able to keep a boyfriend in the last few years. The Professor believed what he was saying…but something still wasn't right.

It was more than William's warning that pricked the hairs on the back of her neck and gave her the sinking feeling that their change in course wasn't correct. She was fairly certain they weren't supposed to be in that particular section. No one else was around; there were only a few mechanized robots moving along the catwalks. The Professor seemed unfazed, loping along as if he knew exactly where he was going. He turned one way

HOLLIN'S HEIR

and then another and, before she knew it, she was hopelessly lost.

"Come along, girl. No dawdling. Your mother's waiting," he blustered, turning again and taking them down a steep ramp, then zigzagging around one corridor and then another before bounding out along another catwalk.

"She's depending on me to get you there, yes, she is."

"My mother's here?" Kricket asked.

"Of course," he answered back, but his words did little to squelch her growing concern.

Xnam had been very definitive that she couldn't ever go back. Kricket wondered briefly if the Professor would want to help her behind their backs. He had known her for her entire life. It would sort of make sense that he would try to reunite her with her mom and help them escape, wouldn't it? She assumed so, but she wasn't sure. William's comment worried her. He'd never been exceptionally good at sign language, and she wondered at his use of it.

"Professor, I—" but she stopped as he came to an abrupt halt in front of her.

He looked around him, the frown on his face deepening as he pulled a small device from the pocket of his jacket and began to scan the air around them. "Should be here by now," he muttered crossly, scanning the air again.

"My mother?" she asked cautiously, but he only turned to glare at her in frustration.

Slowly, she backed up a few steps but bumped into the Nubalah behind her. She turned and regarded him warily. There was no mistaking that he wasn't about to let her past him.

"You mother is already at our destination," the Professor answered as if irritated with her. The device had begun beeping, and he nodded in satisfaction as he spoke. "Thanks to your incredibly stupid attack, Malizore has taken her and plans to publicly execute her unless we deliver you immediately."

"Who's we?" Kricket asked, heart thudding. She hadn't moved, had forced herself to stand perfectly still, but the

CHAPTER SEVEN

Nubalah clamped his arms around her in restraint anyway.

"I have not worked for more than three decades to lose now," the Professor ranted crossly. "None of this would have happened if she'd gone to safety with your brothers, but no....no, she insisted that she had to stay behind until you grew up a little more...now look at the mess we're in."

"My brothers are alive?" Kricket asked incredulously, but he only turned his back to her and continued his rant.

"If you had been male, none of this would have happened...Oh yes, that's the inauguration of the dilemma right there," he continued as if she hadn't spoken. "How that happened, given all the careful—we needed another genetically stable boy, five boys not four, but we got you. No matter though. What's done is done. He refused to take you, didn't want you, and she refused to leave you alone without protection. Stubborn woman said you were too young, and now look."

"What are you saying?" Kricket asked, hardly believing her ears. She liked William's father, had always stood up for him when her mother complained or became frustrated with him. Kricket was never wrong; she always knew what lay beneath the surface of a person.

The Professor turned and strode purposely back to her, stopping less than an inch away from her and leaning his face so close that she could feel the hot exhalation of his breath. "You are not nearly as important as your mother, girl. I'm sorry—I truly am—always liked you, despite you turning out to be a female. But we need Margaret to finish, and you've always been..." He paused and leaned back a little, regarding her curiously.

"What?" she spat back, anger slowly replacing the fear she felt.

"Expendable," He finished, matter-of-factly. "I'm afraid your only value to your father now is to pacify Malizore. I need to prove to both sides that I'm still loyal...at least long enough for—damned inconvenient, that's what it is. Bad timing. Perhaps it's all for the better. Cronus has his son's with Meera's daughter; the plan is coming to fruition. Perhaps…"

Kricket simply stared at him in open-mouthed horror. There were many revelations in what he said, but it was not the Professor's betrayal that hurt. He didn't even care for William, so there was no surprise in the knowledge that he didn't care for her. However, the fact that her brothers weren't dead but had simply left her and her mother alone on a broken planet to die, cut like a knife across her chest. She loved her brothers, had genuinely mourned them.

"There's the signal," the Professor said in exaggerated relief, drawing her thoughts back to her current predicament. "Only a moment now…"

Kricket frantically tried to think of some way to escape. She doubted the Nubalah would be fooled twice. She'd have to think of a different technique to loosen his grip on her. Before she could act, though, she heard a thud and felt him jerk inwardly toward her. Almost instantly his hold on her relaxed and he fell to the floor.

The next few seconds raced by far too quickly for her to process. She turned, saw the guard fall to the ground lifeless, felt the air around her crackle with electricity and something strange pulling her in and out at the same time. She saw another Nubalah jump over him and slam something metallic onto her chest. Then she felt someone else grab hold of her, just as another electrical charge swirled around her and the room disappeared.

The Professor didn't have time to react. The beam had already locked and would pull him off the ship within seconds. He saw the energy blast that had taken the guard out, watched him fall, and then saw another cursed Nubalah dive over him and slap a restraint on the girl, preventing her transport. The large humanoid warrior wasn't, however, able to attach a similar device on him. As the Professor faded from view, he spied his treacherous son, the offspring he never wanted and who had been a burden to him since birth. As he locked hateful eyes with the boy, he said simply, "You'll regret this."

CHAPTER SEVEN

***

Kricket appeared almost instantly in an entirely different room, which was filled with consoles and dozens of people who stopped their work to turn and stare at her. Someone was still behind her, holding on to her, but the warm strength was supportive rather than imprisoning, and she needed it, so she didn't resist. She only had time to blink two or three times and register the sea of curious faces staring at her, before a deep voice ordered them sent back to the medical bay. A second later, she was there.

The second time she emerged, however, she wasn't nearly as surprised by the transport. She shrugged, loosening the man's grip on her, then heaved him over her shoulder and off of her. Caught off guard, he was propelled forward and landed with a thud on the floor of the medical bay. Startled, the staff rushing toward her scattered, then altered their direction to help him.

"Your Highness, are you all right?" Dr. Xnam asked, quickly pulling out a medical scanner and checking for injuries. Turning to Kricket, she added in a chastising tone, "You need to get better at distinguishing who's here to help you versus to kill you."

"How was I supposed to know one thug grabbing me from the next?" she replied frostily. "I'm new here, remember?"

"Thug?" Coltame asked, sitting up and rubbing the spot on his head that had banged against the hard floor. "I've been called a lot things in my life, but never a thug."

Kricket shrugged but was spared the need to reply by William's hasty entrance, followed by several Nubalah warriors. "Are you okay?" he asked, obviously out of breath and very worried.

"I'm fine," she answered, as if nearly being kidnapped were a normal sort of thing. "Just fine really, never better. Why would you ask?"

"The Professor?" Coltame asked, rising from the floor and brushing off the medical team that had begun to hover over him.

"Escaped," Gage answered, stepping through the medical bay doors and taking in the chaotic scene. "She's all right?" he asked in return, jerking his head in Kricket's direction. When the medical technician nodded that her medical scans of the girl were clear, he added, "Then would someone mind filling me in on what's going on?"

"Malizore has my mother," she said suddenly, gaining their attention. "He'll kill her if the Professor doesn't show up with me. Can't anyone do anything to stop him?"

Coltame exchanged a rueful glance with Gage. Malizore had declared himself emperor of the Roan, but he was Rheigan born. There was a very strong chance the girl's mother was already dead— especially if Malizore didn't know her lineage. "Open a channel and propose an exchange," he suggested. "We have several people he wants. That might be enticing enough for him to delay."

Gage carefully weighed his options, then nodded curtly in agreement. "I concur. And I think the captain will agree as well, considering the circumstances." Sliding a security panel open, he keyed the codes necessary to access the bridge and silently tapped in the order to proceed. Then, turning his attention back to the girl, he gave her a genuinely sympathetic look. "If it helps, the Roan are barbaric, but they don't generally waste lives unnecessarily. He won't kill what he can sell; that might buy us a little time."

Coltame turned his head so he didn't have to face the girl. He hadn't lied, but he hadn't told her the truth either. Malizore would have no qualms about carrying out his threats; they both knew the mother was probably executed the moment DeSirpi arrived alone.

A small measure of decorum restored, Coltame regarded Gage evenly. His stature reminded everyone present of his authority, even over the captain of the ship. It was only sheer luck that Gage had been acting captain and had had no reservations about contacting him in the dead of night. He was his cousin, the son of his uncle, and the two had been born

CHAPTER SEVEN

within weeks of each other. They had been brought up on board the *Nadir* with the rest of the crew's children and were every bit as close as brothers.

"My quarters are more secure," Coltame said gruffly, unwilling to discuss the matter openly. The medical bay was safe enough, but his office was better. Listening devices were always everywhere and, even though he trusted his own physician, he wasn't about to trust any more of the staff with her. "Xnam, I'm taking the girl out of the medical bay. You may come and personally see to her in my wing, but no one else; is that clear?"

The Redan nodded serenely in confirmation and, as a group, the staff melted back nervously away from him. They had been charged with keeping the girl safe, and they had failed.

Coltame walked brusquely past them, then motioned to Kricket. "Come," he ordered, gesturing with his hand that she was to exit the still open doorway and follow him.

"Why?" she asked stubbornly, refusing to move, her chin cocked to the side defiantly. As one, the crowd around her seemed to quietly gasp, then everything fell totally silent.

"Excuse me?" Coltame returned, unable to keep the irritation out of his voice. His father was the only one who would dare question him publicly. Reflexively, his jaw clenched and he turned, but something about the set of her wide gray eyes kept him from reprimanding her. She was regarding him exactly as she had in his last vision of her: irritated, frustrated, and needing him to understand what he couldn't comprehend. Her hair was the short bob that the long tresses had melted into, and she stood before him in the strange clothing of her world, her arms exposed and the fabric of her jeans clinging to her legs. If there had been any doubt in his mind that she was the same girl of his vision, it was now gone.

"Why should I trust you any more than anyone else?" Kricket asked waspishly, arms crossed defiantly.

She was scared out of her mind. Nothing made sense. Within the span of an unusually short time, someone had tried to kill her, she'd been forbidden to ever return home, her best friend's father had tried to kidnap her, she'd found out her mother had been taken prisoner and that her brothers weren't dead but alive, and then she'd been summarily kidnapped back. Her mind whirled and, for the first time in her life, she thought she just might faint.

She didn't budge when Coltame stepped up to her, but it surprised her when his eyes softened and he gently lifted her chin with the crook of his finger, turning her face upward until their eyes locked. He regarded her for several long seconds before saying, "Because I'm the one the gods of the garden sent to protect you."

CHAPTER EIGHT

"Where is she?" Maerwynn roared in frustration as the Professor materialized alone. It wasn't often that she lost her composure, but far too much rested on her securing the girl for Malizore. Whirling on the technician in charge of the transport, she snarled, "You said you had a lock on both."

"I'm not sure," he answered in a terrified voice. It wasn't good to fail; people generally didn't survive failing. Malizore himself was asleep, and the girl was to be a surprise for him when he woke. But Maerwynn was no less tolerant than their master, and he could very well be facing his final moments of mortality. "Her signal locked," he squeaked. "I don't understand…Her signal locked."

"Someone alerted the crew," the Professor replied in disgust. He wasn't about to mention that it was his own ignominious son who had sounded the alarm. "They had a Nubalah jump into the beam and strap a restraint on her."

"Malizore will not be pleased," she hissed, turning her ire on the white-haired man in front of her. "You have much to explain, Professor."

"All will be revealed in time," he replied frostily. "Your master's impatience will have the empire crawling down our backs anytime now. Goman himself is rumored to have left Syphlein and is scheduled to rendezvous with the *Nadir*."

"Goman?" Maerwynn returned in astonishment, anger dissolving almost instantaneously. "Surely that ancient relic has long since passed to dust."

It was a wasted insult, said more to buy her time to recover from the news than anything else. The emperor's vizier was rumored to have harnessed the power of the gods themselves and would probably live forever. The thought of him leaving the capitol and voyaging to the ends of the known territories was terrifying to her. It meant the emperor himself had ordered him to do so, which meant the emperor had shifted his gaze in their direction.

"What could possibly bring Goman here?" she added cautiously, but she already knew. The emperor had discovered what they had tried to hide for decades and was mobilizing to prevent it.

"The girl is Hollin's granddaughter," the Professor answered bitterly. "A fact that will be well known all across the universe when the information channels wake people up in the standard morning hours. How Jaget put the pieces together so quickly, completely baffles me," he ranted, dissolving once again into his manic state. "The woman you're holding and threatening to execute is Hollin's daughter by Meera."

Maerwynn gasped, eyes widening; she couldn't help it. She'd been so focused on retrieving the girl she hadn't thought to consider that she might be part of the small colony. But how was she to know? She'd wanted to surprise Malizore, catapult herself back into his favor.

"Cronus wants Margaret back," the Professor continued in his ranting manner. "Why do you think he ordered me to expose myself and deliver the girl? You were threatening to kill the only one who can translate her father's journals and, without those translations, we'll never find the locations of the original keys.

CHAPTER EIGHT

Without those keys, it's plan B: smaller, weaker, less impressive. Your master will be well pleased when he finds himself settling for that, oh yes, he will."

"What is your current strategy then?" she replied carefully, eyes narrowing. If the Professor had bothered to tell her who the girl was, she could have been spared the near humiliation of almost executing the mother. It was his fault. He had purposely withheld critical information, lied to her by saying the girl was a local of no consequence—and she would not soon forget it.

"Barter her," he spat in return. "Jaget will open up diplomatic relations by morning...or that mixed-blooded son of Rastmus will. Cronus has already left Aelis; he'll be here within hours. You'll trade both Margaret and me for Tral and San. Jaget's sure to tell them I was the one who tried to give you the girl, but he'll have to work that out on his own, yes, he will; can't be helped now. No one else could have gotten her out but me, and that didn't even work, did it? The important thing is to get Margaret back to him and get her translating those damnable logs before Goman docks and discovers they exist."

"Malizore will not appreciate your return to Cronus's camp," She hissed dangerously. Just whose side the Professor was on was yet to be determined, but if the mother was who the Professor said she was, and Goman himself was in transit to the *Nadir*, then she had to proceed with caution. "Why not use her here?" she suggested silkily. "We have the copies you provided us with. Cronus has his own agenda. We have her, and we can utilize her just as easily as he can."

"Because she trusts Cronus and knows damn well how her father felt about your master," he returned. "And Cronus will cry holy outrage and bring the eyes of all the Delsheni Senate down upon us. Do you honestly want that kind of exposure? He'll have the entire fleet here within days, and we'll have far more than just one battleship looking into our business. The emperor already suspects or he wouldn't have sent Goman; he'd have sent Itin or Trask or even Rastmus. Instead, he's sent Goman, which means he's ready to openly play his hand. He could have the entire armada here within days, and then where would three decades of work be? Eh? The emperor will have Hollin's keys, and the Guardian will be his. His enemies will cease to exist, just as before."

"Very well," she concurred reluctantly. She was not about to let the Professor order her around, but, by choosing his plan, he could take the fall if it failed. Malizore was already angry with him, and it wouldn't take much to shift the blame in his direction. "But if you double cross Malizore again, DeSirpi, all that will be left of your life's work will be ash and ruin."

The Professor stopped his pacing and stared at the woman the Roan laughingly called a general. Malizore's mistress—that's all she was and would ever be. She was dangerous though, and he knew it. Plan B had failed, and with any luck plan C would figure itself out quickly enough to see him safely returned to Aelis. Damned girl; damned boy. Damn them both.

***

"Would someone please explain to me what's going on?" Kricket asked. Fatigue was setting in, and fear was dissolving into anger and frustration.

A small army of Nubalah had escorted them from the medical bay, through a maze of hallways, and up an elevator to a long, private hallway with four doors on each side. On either side of the elevator, both at the entrance and the exit, were armored guards, and each door of the hallway was guarded with two Nubalah. It should have made her feel safe, but it didn't; it only brought home that she was in a strange place and didn't know what was happening to her.

She had been led to the first doorway and ushered through to an ornately decorated room in which there was honestly nothing in her experience to compare to. Rich, heavily embroidered fabrics lined the ceiling and the walls, held in place by ornate and sparkling metal medallions of varying sizes. The floor was also different from that of the medical bay or even the hallways

CHAPTER EIGHT

of the ship. It was thickly padded and carpeted in a contrasting color to the draperies. The furniture was a deep-colored wood of some sort, arranged in a semicircle around the small room as if for a large conference. As her eyes glanced past the windows, she realized the scenery portrayed outside was not that of space or the planet below but of the predawn hours of a strange cityscape full of gothic-looking, museum-like, white stone buildings. It was a few minutes before she realized they weren't windows at all, but screens portraying the images one would expect to see outside a window.

"Has William had a chance to speak with you at all?" Coltame asked, opening the conversation. The girl was obviously frightened and confused, but there was no doubt she was a fighter. His back and shoulder ached from being tossed onto the floor, and he rubbed the pulled muscles in his arm absently as he regarded her.

He still wasn't sure how she'd done it. The Nubalah could do things like that, but they were massively large and well-muscled humanoids. She was tiny, no larger than a child of a dozen years, and he was much heavier and broader. Yet he had been flipped up and over before he'd even known what was happening.

"No," she answered simply, eyes regarding him cautiously in return.

He glanced automatically at the boy, but he had shrunk in his seat, looking even more uncomfortable than he had before. They were all tired, but, given the night's nearly disastrous turn of events, he didn't consider it prudent to wait any longer. He would also rather not have had his initial conversation with her in the presence of his cousin, but Gage was technically the acting captain until the graveyard shift ended, and the Professor's near abduction had happened on his watch.

Glancing around to see that everyone was seated comfortably, he began, "My name is Coltame. I am the son of Rastmus, who is the son of the Emperor Zoujin." Then, nodding in the direction of his cousin, he added, "This is Lieutenant Commander Gage. He is the acting captain of this ship until the night shift ends."

He paused and Kricket nodded that she understood. "Do you understand why you're here?"

She slowly shook her head no.

"Did you ever know your grandfather, your mother's father?" he asked, taking a different track.

Kricket nodded her head cautiously yes, then frowned in confusion, perplexed by a topic she hadn't expected. "My grandfather?" she asked. "Why?"

"Did you know him well?" he asked, more casually than he felt.

"He died just over four years ago," she responded, caught off guard and still not sure what her grandfather had to do with things.

"So you knew him?" he asked, trying to stay neutral and conceal his excitement. He suddenly felt like a young boy, the largest part of him dying to know if the legends were true and discover what had happened to the legendary hero.

"Of course. He lived with us my whole life," she answered simply, in a confused tone.

"What can you tell me about him?" he coaxed, but she only shrugged and gave him a strange look that suggested she wasn't sure what he wanted to know.

She shifted in her chair, not sure what to say, where to begin, or even why he'd want to know. She'd loved her grandfather very much. Growing up with a single mother, he was the only father she'd honestly ever known. His death had been hard on her and, even now, several years later, she had to struggle with the emotions that always rose to the surface when she remembered him. There was so much she could say, but she wasn't sure she could form the words to say it.

"His name was George Holland," she began uncertainly. "He died when I was fourteen."

Coltame watched her carefully, trying to determine if she was being intentionally vague or if she simply didn't know what he wanted to hear. She had been through an incredible ordeal, so it was entirely possible that she was just exhausted and hadn't

CHAPTER EIGHT

fully recovered yet.

"We knew him as Giagous Hollin, or Hollin," he supplied, watching the astonished reactions of both his cousin and the Professor's son, but focusing mainly on the girl. "He was the son of the Emperor Elgar and the older half-brother of our current Emperor Zoujin; he was very famous."

Kricket sat up a little straighter in her chair, interested and yet wary at the same time. Her grandfather? It had to be some sort of misunderstanding. Her grandfather had been larger than life to her, but he'd been a retired military veteran on her home world—a world that still maintained extraterrestrials didn't exist, despite the current invasion. He'd smoked cigars, watched sports, and snuck out with her to eat fast food when her mother wasn't looking. He couldn't have been from another planet. Could he?

"Did he tell you anything about where he came from or what he did before arriving on the colony?" Coltame asked as gently as he could. He wasn't used to mincing words. Rheigans didn't employ mediation and negotiation techniques. They demanded what they needed to know, threatened when they had to, and always carried out their threats. The girl was different though. He needed, wanted, to be in her good graces. It was an unusual and rather complicated situation for him to navigate.

When the girl merely shook her head in a negative gesture, he sighed heavily and re-grouped his thoughts. "Was the Professor aware of her lineage?" he asked William.

"I don't know," William said uncomfortably, giving Kricket an apologetic look. "I was never in his confidence. I mean, other than to hand him things or run errands, he rarely ever noticed me. I didn't even know Kricket and the boys were—"

"Boys?" Coltame interrupted, far more harshly than he intended to. He sat straight up in his chair, giving William his full attention. If there were grandsons, that changed everything.

"Kricket's brothers. They were killed in the first attack of the Roan. A lot of the colonists were," William supplied meekly. "I thought you knew that."

"No they weren't," Kricket contradicted softly, fighting the tears that suddenly threatened to spill out over her eyes. She was tired and hurt, and the emotional roller coaster she'd been riding threatened to overwhelm her at any second. She didn't know what any of this had to do with why she'd been brought here. She wanted to know why the Professor, who she had trusted, had been taking her to Malizore. She wanted to know what would happen to her now that there was no exchange being made. She wanted to know what was happening to her mother. She wanted to know why her brothers had abandoned her, why she wasn't worth taking too.

"They weren't?" William squeaked, nearly jumping out of his chair to face her. He'd attended their memorial, helped to pack up their things, held Kricket's hand while she grieved and her mother had grown increasingly detached from her. His father had lamented their loss, had been cross for days at the waste of it all.

"Your father said they weren't," Kricket continued in a dull voice. They had gone away and left her behind. The thought was crushing, and the heartache she felt was every bit as strong as the day she'd been told they'd died. She looked up at the dark-haired man who was questioning her and wondered briefly if she should say anything more or if she should keep it to herself. She didn't care anymore, she decided; it didn't matter anyway. She had nowhere else to go and no idea who to trust anymore. William was the only thing in her life that was familiar, and if he'd thrown his allegiance in with the men before her, then she would also.

"While we were on the catwalk, he said that none of this would have happened if my mother had left with my brothers, but she stayed...because of me. He said Malizore had her, and he wanted me in exchange. I was expendable—she wasn't," she added bitterly.

"How many boys?" Gage asked incredulously, unable to stop himself. Hollin's descendants: the thought was mind-boggling. The sons of Hollin had finally been discovered, and he was a

CHAPTER EIGHT

witness to it. It sent chills up his spine and his heart thudding in anticipation.

"Four," Kricket answered softly, watching the reaction of the men around her. It was obvious there was a lot she didn't know. Part of her was shutting down with the weight of it all, but the bigger part of her was curious to know what had been kept from her.

"Four boys?" Coltame asked in awe, hardly believing what he was hearing. "All from one mother?"

The odds of that were impossible. Human females simply didn't have that kind of capacity anymore; it had been bred out of them. A man was incredibly lucky to receive one living child from a single female. Male or female, if you could produce a living heir, your status in society skyrocketed. For a Rheigan to produce four male heirs, even if they were grandsons produced through a daughter, was a marvel that simply never happened without a plethora of wives and medical intervention.

He couldn't help the innate reaction the news produced in him. The girl's mother had birthed five living children; the daughter was a gold mine. If he had simply wanted her before, he coveted her now with all the ferociousness of his Rheigan heritage.

"My mother had seven children," Kricket clarified, and watched in amazement as the two strange men in front of her nearly fell out of their seats. "I'm the next to the youngest. My next older brother died when he was four. I don't know why, — no one would ever tell me—and then my younger brother…" Kricket paused and mentally recalled the chubby baby she barely remembered. "He had problems," she finished cryptically. The boy had been born with several serious health problems, but she'd never actually understood why he'd died.

"Problems?" Coltame asked, curious despite himself.

"Genetic variances not necessarily conducive with long-term survival," William explained, then blushed deeply when all eyes turned to him.

"Four living sons of Hollin…" Gage marveled, changing the

subject and trying to steer the conversation back in the direction it had been going. The storytellers would have a field day when they learned that. There were many who would welcome the news that Hollin had four descendants to carry on his legacy. Cautiously he stole a glance at his cousin. Coltame was three quarters Delsheni, but he was his father's only son and loyal to the emperor. The first thing he would do would be to contact Syphlein with the news.

"Grandsons," Kricket clarified, drawing attention back to her. "My mother was an only child."

"It doesn't matter," Coltame explained. "In our culture, sons and grandsons are the same. The patriarch is always given credit for the progeny, even several generations removed."

"But if they're mongrels..." Gage offered hesitantly, wondering if maybe they would stand a better chance if their ancestry was tarnished a bit. The colony the girl had been found on was listed but not recognized. That meant they were interbreeding with the general population of mixed bloods.

"We've already established that Kricket isn't," Coltame returned, immediately correcting what others were sure to assume as well.

"Then who's the father?" Gage asked, pondering the possibilities out loud. "A descendant of the crew who worked with Hollin? Perhaps they went into exile with him."

"Xnam's working on it now," the prince offered. "We should know in another few hours. She's three quarters Delsheni, directly from Azill's line; that's prolific enough to offer a plethora of possibilities."

Gage nodded in an understanding that Kricket was denied. She knew she was on a Delsheni ship, knew the dark man seated across from her was not Delsheni but a Rheigan, the controlling power, but how she played into those facts baffled her. It was frustrating. They were playing a game with her life that she didn't know the rules to, and she was helplessly at their mercy.

"The Professor said that Cronus has his son's with Meera's daughter," she offered, watching closely as all three men in the

CHAPTER EIGHT

room snapped to attention and stared at her. "Could he be our father? I mean, I never knew him, mom never said anything about him, but if my brothers are his boys-"

"Cronus?" Coltame nearly growled, eyes narrowing and becoming frighteningly dark and dangerous. "Are you positive?"

"He said Cronus has his son's with Meera's daughter. That he needed five boys not four," she clarified, needing her own answer to that cryptic fact. The tension in the room had suddenly increased exponentially. Coltame appeared ready to strangle someone, and William looked terrified that it might be him.

"Coltame..." Gage murmured anxiously, the implications of what the girl had said causing him to forget that this was no casual conversation, like his cousin had tried to create earlier, but an official inquiry to the night's events. "Five boys...five boys of Hollin...a family of five boys...five crafts of the Guardian uniting into one. That's exactly what the legend says."

"What does he mean?" Kricket asked, sitting up a little straighter as the prince seemed to crouch in preparation for an attack on William.

"War," Coltame growled, his eyes dangerously black.

CHAPTER NINE

"Where is it?" Coltame demanded, the ferocity of his dark eyes focused solely on the Professor's son. The words had been said in a low, deadly tone, but the threat behind them was so harsh that he might as well have shouted them. "If Cronus needed five boys from Hollin's line, he knew where it was. Tell me where the Guardian is hidden."

"I don't know!" William wailed, slinking down in his seat and looking more terrified than Kricket had ever seen him. "I swear on my own soul, I don't know…I didn't know the general was…I mean I knew he was out of favor, that he was hiding his family. There are dozens like him in the colony. My father never included me on important discussions…I was nothing to him. I swear."

"Leave him alone," Kricket warned in the same low tone the prince had used, and when he turned his attention to her, his cold eyes met with an equally harsh and challenging glare.

She was sitting forward in her seat, as if she was readying herself to spring forward and intercept any physical attack he might initiate against the boy. The unexpected fierceness of it

CHAPTER NINE

made him pause; his eyes regarded her curiously.

Head to toe, she was esthetically the epitome of a Delsheni female, with her soft-colored eyes and delicate, petite stature. A docile little dove to be petted and indulged. Yet behind her eyes she was no submissive female to be coddled. She was genuinely ready to attack him, he realized with a start. It was not what anyone would have expected and, for the first time, he wondered if the mutilation of Malizore had been as accidental as everyone presumed. His cousin had noticed the dichotomy as well and turned a curious and speculative glance in his direction.

Slowly, Coltame relaxed his shoulders and, although his posture continued to maintain his authority in the room, he sat back in his chair and softened the look on his face to a more diplomatic neutral. In response, she echoed his movements, also backing down, but her posture remained taut, silently letting him know she'd fight him if she had to.

He loved it. In his experience, females simply didn't do that. Those of the matriarchal courts would of course, but few of those were as pretty as the girl before him. She had absolutely no idea how seductive he found it.

"Where is the Sentinel Guardian?" He asked her in an even tone, impressing himself with his ability to control his anger and yet maintain control of the situation.

"What's a Sentinel Guardian?" she countered, although he could tell she wasn't entirely ignorant on the subject. Something about the name had triggered a look of recognition in her eyes, and her face appeared wary and alert.

"A war machine," he supplied. "Depending on your political beliefs, your grandfather either saved it or stole it."

Kricket shook her head, trying to clear the whirlwind of thoughts that assaulted her on all sides. The men in the room stared at her expectantly, but she didn't have the answer they wanted. The vision said it was time for the guardian, but she didn't know anything about war machines. Her grandfather had spoiled her, not educated her on military matters or expected her to follow her brothers. He'd enrolled her in martial arts because her determination to keep up with the boys amused him. He'd included her in their paintball games and hunting trips for the same reasons, often chiding his grandsons that she was tougher and had more fire than the lot of them. There had been nothing about a war machine...Or had there? She tried desperately to tie half-remembered comments and activities into place, but the answer eluded her.

"He never said anything about a war machine," she answered, shaking her head again and clearing her thoughts. "He wanted the boys in the military, trained them, coached them, but he was a retired army general. They always knew they were destined for the service; it's what our family did."

Gage sat back in his chair with a sigh and rubbed his eyes with his hands. He had never been in a position of authority during a critical hour, and a nervousness began to settle around him that he didn't like. Hollin's granddaughter was sitting in a chair in front of him—unfathomable. She had four living brothers-unimaginable. He took a deep breath to calm his racing heart and clear his mind. She had revealed that Cronus was involved. That he had needed five boys. Just how was the infamous Delsheni Senator Cronus involved in this? He wondered silently. It was well known that Cronus had led the movement for the Delsheni to secede from the Rheigan empire. Could the girl and her brothers actually be fathered by the old man? The idea was mind-boggling and disturbing at the same time. Just how far would a man go to secure his own power?

"We have to protect her," Gage said after a few seconds of silence. "I understand that the empire isn't going to be happy, but she's not her brothers, and she appears genuinely ignorant of this. There seems to be more in play here than the simple revelation of Hollin's fate—if that can be considered simple. It's not just the Professor or Malizore. If Kricket is correct that Senator Cronus is part of the equation and it's exposed that she's Hollin's granddaughter daughter through the maternal line— wait, Meera?" he asked, suddenly remembering Kricket's words and comparing them to the legends and stories he'd been told.

CHAPTER NINE

"She said, Cronus has his son's with Meera's daughter. Wasn't Hollin supposed to have fallen in love with Princess Meera, the empress Avala's daughter? I'm sure I read something about that somewhere. I know Avala testified that Meera died in an accident just after Hollin was exiled, but wasn't there was also a lot of speculation she vanished with him? Leary protect her if she's Hollin's granddaughter through Meera! Kricket's mother and children would have a better claim to the old Delsheni imperial throne than almost anyone else in the known universe. That has to be why Cronus is involved."

Coltame sat back in his seat with a forceful exhalation of breath. Never, in a million years, would he have expected the conversation to turn in the direction it had. "Let's not allow imaginations and fancy to cloud the facts we already know," he advised sternly. But the ideas Gage proposed unsettled him, and he would ask Xnam to confirm or discount them as soon as possible. Meera had been the old Emperor Azill's daughter—not a granddaughter—a daughter of the man who many considered the rightful ruler. Not only that, Meera had also been the daughter of his former empress. Azill had become emperor by marrying his wife, the daughter of the previous emperor. If Gage's speculations were true, the girl's line had a better claim to the Delsheni throne than Cronus himself, and, arguably, better than either of Azill's recognized grandsons and their descendants.

The gods were indeed cruel pranksters. If his cousin was right, the empire would not welcome what they had discovered, and the girl would, indeed, be in considerable danger. He wondered silently if that was why the gods had sent her to him. If it was true, the political backlash was going to be huge.

With a groan, he realized he would never be allowed to permanently keep the girl, and any temporary alliance he'd just gotten his father to approve of would be in serious jeopardy when he found out. If she was Cronus's biological daughter, if she was Meera's granddaughter, then, despite her Rheigan ancestry through Hollin, she was about as purebred a Delsheni royal as existed in modern times. Her children would be considered Azill's progeny. There wasn't a Rheigan alive who would allow her offspring anywhere near the throne.

"Four boys of Hollin," Gage added, looking directly at his cousin. "Four boys possibly related to Cronus and Meera."

"I know," Coltame responded grimly, sighing heavily and regarding the occupants of the room.

"If it's true, Cronus is going to want her back," Gage determined. "Perhaps fate has made the decision of her destiny for us."

"No," Coltame answered, more gruffly than he'd intended, causing his cousin and the others to regard him curiously. "Other arrangements have already been made."

"What arrangements?" Kricket asked hesitantly, her stomach sinking. Adrenaline suddenly shot through her body, but, again, she wasn't sure if it was from fear or some ethereal warning that her life was about to change forever.

Coltame paused, unwilling to reveal his father's conversation in mixed company, but his fear that his patriarch would renege floated front and center of his thoughts. Strangely it never dawned on him to rethink his decision. If anything, he was more determined than ever. Given the circumstances, every logical reasoning demanded that he should withdraw and give her up, but he simply couldn't do it. If he was going to proceed though, he had to act quickly.

"Cronus will have already made provisions for her," Gage contended. He understood the empire wouldn't be happy with the turn of events, but surely his cousin wouldn't hold the girl accountable. Then again, they might just confiscate her; who knew how a Rheigan rationalized.

"By order of my father, she is to enter into a one-year contractual alliance with me," Coltame responded impassively, but his heart was thudding in his chest as he spoke. Dumbfounded, his cousin and William could only stare at him in response.

"What does that mean?" Kricket asked hesitantly, not entirely

CHAPTER NINE

sure she liked where the conversation was going. "What does he mean by 'one-year alliance'?"

"Marriage," William squeaked incredulously.

"Like hell!" Kricket spat, regaining her wits. Fists balled and ready to fight, she stood in defiance. "No. Absolutely not. You people are insane, you know that? I'm not getting married to someone I've never met before."

"Kricket, this isn't home," William blurted out unexpectedly, surprising himself. *I swore my allegiance to the prince and the empire,* he thought ruefully, *promised I would take on the responsibility to educate her in what would be expected of her.* Now he supposed he would have to fulfill that duty. "Things are done differently here than at home. I haven't had time to explain, but I promise I will. It's about alliances, nothing more. Trust me, if you're really Cronus's daughter, you're going to need Prince Coltame's help. Cronus isn't someone you want to go up against alone; even I know that," he supplied, silently adding that the old senator had been the bane of his father's existence. If his father had been afraid of him, that was a good enough reason for him to be too.

Coltame regarded the exchange blackly, displeased and irritated by the girl's response. Half the women in the empire would have jumped at the chance of a one-year alliance with him. Rejection was a novel and not entirely pleasant feeling. He was risking everything to abide by the instructions of his vision, yet she was responding as if she was being saddled with some distasteful blaggard who was unworthy of her. But then again, he mused silently, she didn't know anything about him or the situation she found herself in.

"I don't need protecting," she fired back rudely. "Not that way anyhow."

"Yes, you do," Coltame insisted evenly, surprising her and everyone else in the room. "Kricket, it's a matter of safety, not proliferation," he added and, when she turned to him with a speculative glance, added, "I promise you I won't…" He paused, considering his words given the mixed audience watching them.

"You are to be given into my care for the period of one year. In that time, you will be expected to learn about our society and the expectations you must live up to based upon the position you now find yourself in. You have my word that I will not expect...that, given the situation, there will be no inappropriate demands made," he finished, glaring at his cousin, who had begun chuckling. "You will have your own quarters, and I will respect your privacy."

"And what do you get out of this arrangement?" she asked pointedly, eyes boring into him.

He was a little taken aback by the question. If he was truthful with himself, he honestly didn't get much at all. He got a delay in the other negotiations being carried on, but certainly nothing more. She had no dowry, although none was actually expected in a short-term contract, and she had no family alliances to bring other than she was the granddaughter of a traitor and the apparent illegitimate daughter of one of the most despised Delsheni politicians the empire had ever known. If anything, he had far more to lose than gain. He was moving forward on nothing except an assumed command he'd been given in a vision, which he couldn't even prove was legitimate.

"Leave us," he commanded in a low but stern voice. His cousin seemed surprised, and the Professor's son cautious, but both he and William rose obediently. With respectful nods to both the prince and Kricket, they left the room without question. For several long seconds, he stared at her, mulling over his thoughts and wondering what he should say, if anything, then finally stood and added, "Come with me."

Kricket slowly rose and did as she was told, but with far more guardedness than she had shown with the Professor. She didn't know this man, yet the others apparently did as he commanded without question; so she followed their lead.

As she trailed behind him through a hidden side panel and into a small living space, caution niggled at the back of her neck and down her spine. It was less ornately furnished than the conference room, with a focus more on comfort than on making

CHAPTER NINE

an impression, yet she had no doubt that the furnishings were expensive and still reflected his wealth and status.

"These are my personal living quarters," he confirmed and then merely stood there, giving her an expectant look.

Kricket wasn't sure what she was supposed to do—and terribly afraid of what she might be expected to do—so she merely nodded, eyes wide and guarded, then hesitantly looked around. It actually wasn't much more than a small, square room. There was a sunken area lined by, what appeared to be, three long couches forming a U shape, which faced another artificial window programmed to show a garden scene. Three long, narrow steps allowed access down to the couches below and, when seated, the arrangement gave the illusion of being able to step up and through to the gardens beyond.

Glancing more closely at the window scene, she suddenly had an inexplicably odd sensation of déjà vu. The colors were not nearly as perfect as the pervious window scenes—they seemed a bit faded and muted—but nothing could detract from its splendor. It was framed by beautifully manicured trees and shrubbery, giving the illusion that you were stealing a peek at the manicured lawns and crystal lakeside beyond. Entranced, she stepped around the sunken sofas and pressed a cautious hand to the screen. To her surprise, it gave way easily, wrapping around her fingertips like silk fabric, the colors enclosing around her hand like a rainbow chrysalis.

"Do you like it?"

She could hardly find the words to respond. "Where is this place?" she asked breathlessly, confusion swirling in her mind. It was an exact replica of the garden she had traveled to in her dreams since childhood, but how a dream world could be depicted with such perfect accuracy rendered her speechless in both fright and wonder.

"It was destroyed by the Trogoul nearly a century ago," he said softly, and when she turned to him in surprise, he added, "I believe this is the only recording of its kind. Viewers like this had only just been created, and recorded scenes from that time are very rare. One full planetary year of seasons. The final year before it was obliterated."

"But why?" she asked, visibly upset by the idea. "Why would they destroy it?"

"Because it was located on the grounds of the Delsheni Imperial Palace. It was first cultivated over a thousand years before by the Emperor Xsan as a tribute to the goddess Leary."

"Leary?" she asked, a small frown knotting her forehead. The name seemed so familiar, yet she was sure she'd never heard it before.

"Leary or Ilearia. She's the goddess of luck and prosperity," he supplied, walking toward her and staring at the idyllic scene. "More specifically, the goddess of luck while in love and the prosperity after. Her husband, Irage, is the god of military stratagem and victory. Legends say they shared a great, forbidden love that, in the end anyway, even the rulers of the gods couldn't deny them."

When she simply stared at him, he stepped forward and gently removed her hand, which was perilously close to tearing his precious screen. "They are the only two gods that both the Delsheni and the Rheigans share in common, and, by tradition, we recognize them as our originating ancestors. Xsan built the garden after Leary came to him in a dream. It's supposedly an exact copy of the garden she built for Irage beyond the gates of Annon when he was banished from the mortal world for tricking the god of pestilence into infecting himself with his own poison. Legend stated that as long as the garden stood, the old Delsheni Empire would prosper, so the Trogoul destroyed it to dishearten the people, and, sure enough, the empire fell."

"To the Rheigans," she supplied, connecting the bits and pieces she already knew. Gently, but firmly, she removed her hand from his and crossed her arms protectively in front of her.

"Not at first," he explained. "Your grandfather uncovered Xsan's logs and went on a quest to resurrect the Guardian. He used it to drive back the Trogoul, but the old empire still floundered under the Delsheni Emperor Azill. The Rheigan

CHAPTER NINE

armies were able to take control, but the people offered little resistance, and there was very little blood spilled. They wanted protection from the Trogoul and later from Malizore and his Roan."

"Why didn't the Rheigans rebuild it?" she asked. "Don't they worship Leary as well?"

"Because it stood for Delsheni rule," he clarified. "The emperor forbade its cultivation. Humanity serves a new empire now. He moved the capital to Syphlein, in the heart of Rheigan space, and built a new Imperial Palace."

"But you're Rheigan...right?" she countered. "Why keep a recording of Delsheni gardens in your quarters?"

Coltame gave small, wistful smile, his eyes slightly sheepish. "I prefer to think of them as Leary's gardens. She seems to have taken a mysterious interest in me throughout my life, and I keep it in deference to her and her continued goodwill." He paused as if uncomfortable, then admitted, "But I turn it off when others are around. My mother is the youngest half-sister of the captain, and, if she or my cousins or visitors entered this room, they would see the great rust-colored mountains of the Syphlein capitol or a modern scene from the Imperial Palace."

"Then why show it to me?" she asked guardedly, eyes narrowing.

"Would you care to sit?" he asked, his hand indicating the sunken couches. "I don't have many beverages suitable for a lady, but I'm sure I could find you something." When she shook her head, declining his offer, he breathed a heavy sigh and seemed to flounder for a moment. After a few uneasy seconds, he turned and descended the steps to the couches below them anyway. "There's not an easy answer," he admitted uncomfortably, casually taking a seat and making himself comfortable. "But it has a great deal to do with you."

"Me?" she asked, bewildered, but he simply nodded and indicated again that she take a seat. Despite herself, she was curious and obliged him, yet made sure to take a seat that left as much space as possible between them.

"Years ago, Leary blessed me with glimpses into the garden—her garden—which can only be seen through dreams and visions," he began. "I was never very adept with the Sight, but what few visions I've been given over the years were very clear."

Kricket shifted uneasily in her seat, her eyes leaving the prince and turning toward the recording. She'd had visions of the garden too. For what seemed her entire life, her dreams had carried her there. What she experienced, what she saw, always came true...She just never knew when or how it would happen.

"There was only ever one consistency, besides the garden itself of course," he continued as she turned back to face him. "And that was you."

"Me?" she asked again, dumfounded and slightly panicked.

"You recognize the garden, don't you," he returned, more of a statement than a question. When she nodded hesitantly, he added seriously, "In my last vision of you in the garden, I was told to find you. My instructions were very clear. I was to marry you and keep you safe. If I refused or didn't obey that command..." He paused and closed his eyes, the image of her falling to the ground as clear as the morning he'd witnessed it on the ship's official log. "I saw the destruction of the garden by the Roan; I saw you fall from Malizore's hands exactly as it came to life the other morning on the security screen. I'm not a religious man, nor am I a young boy prone to silly fantasies. I honestly believe this is no coincidence and that Leary has brought you to me in order to keep you safe, but from what or whom, I don't know yet."

Kricket turned her head, unable to look at either him or the scenic view of the garden. She'd had the same vision. The garden was dead; there was no going back.

"I have no reason for proceeding other than my beliefs in this otherworldly message. Beliefs which..." he admitted in a low tone, "haven't always been as strong as they should be." He paused slightly, then continued. "Please, understand that this is awkward for me as well. I'm not used to this kind of exposure to

CHAPTER NINE

my thoughts. But this I know: if you are truly Cronus's daughter, in conjunction with Hollin's offspring, you must believe me when I tell you that you are not safe, and the gods would have just reasons to assign you a protector. I am not my grandfather the emperor, nor am I my father, who is very high in his internal cabinet. But Leary seems to have sent you to me in the belief that I can look after you. Therefore I offer you what limited security I can for as long as the gods decree me a worthy protector."

"Right..." she responded slowly in return, the sarcasm evident. "The gods told you."

Either he was nuts or she'd hit her head harder than she thought. Still, he knew about the garden, and she hadn't told anyone about it. There was no way he could have known. It was all terribly strange and confusing.

"You recognize the garden," he returned softly, eyes holding hers. "I doubt anyone has ever shown you actual images of it before today, and yet you know it. Do you not know me as well?"

Slowly she shook her head back and forth in a negative gesture. There had always been so many people to visit with in the garden; almost all of their dreamlike details remained fuzzy afterward. She could have met him, wanted what he said to be true, but she had no waking memory of him.

Coltame sighed, genuinely disappointed. Rising, he accessed a panel from the wall and retrieved a small, metal tablet. He read the contents briefly for a few minutes, then placed his hand, palm down, on the screen. Scanning it a second time, he took a deep breath, returned to the couch, and took a seat next to her.

"This is the contract," he said simply. "I'm taking a leap of faith, just as you are, and I'm asking you to trust me that my intentions in offering you this alliance are honorable. If Cronus is involved, there's no time for courtships. Once my father discovers that you are possibly his biological offspring, all bets are off; he'll refuse to allow me to have anything to do with you, and you'll be on your own."

Silently he handed the tablet to her, but she could only stare at it numbly. For the millionth time, she wished the innate feelings that had guided her almost all her life would assist her on demand, but she felt nothing. She believed him when he said he wanted to help her, but she had also believed the Professor, and that had almost meant her execution.

"Do you think my mother's already dead?" she asked, her heart heavy and her voice threatening to break.

Coltame lowered the tablet, his eyes following it downward to his knees. "Not if she's told him she's Hollin's daughter, or, perhaps, if the Professor was given enough time to explain the situation, or if Malizore bothered to listen to the *Nadir*'s request to open communications with us."

"What are the chances of that?" she asked, hopeful, yet realizing even as she asked that her mother was probably already dead and that it was her fault.

"Not good," he said honestly, then wished he hadn't as giant tears escaped her eyes, and she sucked in a small hiccup of despair.

He wasn't good with crying females. He never quite knew what to do with them besides send them back to their rooms and ignore them until they'd regained their composure. If he was going to take charge of her, however, he supposed he'd have to do something, but, watching her as the tears flowed heavier, he honestly wasn't sure what. Hesitantly he placed his hand on her shoulder and patted it clumsily, but that was of little help.

Standing, he once again left the circle of couches and returned with a small hand towel. "Here," he offered lamely, sitting back down beside her and handing her the absorbent cloth.

"It's my fault," she said miserably, taking the towel and roughly wiping the tears from her face. "If only I'd gone straight back to the shelter instead of looking for William. The day was so beautiful…It hadn't been a really nice day in months. I didn't even get to say good-bye to her," she finished, the tears making a heavy reappearance.

CHAPTER NINE

Coltame honestly didn't know what to do. Perhaps it was her youth, perhaps she was simply female, or perhaps she was trying to confide in him. Awkwardly he placed his arm across her back as his mother had done to him when he was small, and, to his surprise, she leaned in to his shoulder, face buried into the small towel. But the tears seemed to increase instead of decrease. After what seemed an excruciatingly long time, the sobbing ceased, and she lay quietly against his shoulder, saying nothing, simply pressing against him, which was entirely inappropriate, but honestly rather nice.

***

Goman watched as the clock counted down the hours until his rendezvous with the *Nadir*. He placed Rastmus's report carefully to the side, locking its contents inside the reader so that none but he could access it. His son was to bond himself to the girl in a short-term contract until her loyalty could be assured. It was an odd twist of events and one that he hadn't seen coming, which surprised him.

Rastmus was only half Rheigan blood, his son three quarters Delsheni. If the girl was truly Hollin's granddaughter by Meera, the emperor was not going to be pleased with the match at all—unless…

A slow, delighted smile crossed his face, and the muscles of his neck and shoulders relaxed. Perhaps there was a way to spin the tide in his master's favor and yet stay true to Hollin's legacy after all.

CHAPTER TEN

"I'm sorry," Kricket said quietly, wiping the tears from her face, but she didn't move from him. Instead she sniffed loudly and wrapped her arms around him, pressing her cheek against the side of his chest and absorbing the warmth and the comfort he seemed to give. It had been far too long since anyone had provided her with a shoulder to cry on, and it felt good to let go of all the emotions she'd kept bottled up inside. "I haven't cried since I was told my brothers died," she offered lamely. "I guess I was due."

He wasn't sure what to say in return; it was a new experience for him. Parents sometimes cuddled their children when they were upset, but he was not a parent, and he knew females were inexplicably prone to tears at the oddest times, but he'd never been one to sit and listen to them. It was certainly one of the more awkward situations he'd found himself in. There were highly specific guidelines for dealing with young, unmarried females, and none of them included being alone, in his living quarters, with his arms around her. If anyone were to walk in on them, clothed or not, he'd be honor bound to marry her, which

CHAPTER TEN

would, he mused, solve the problem of getting her to willingly sign the agreement on her own.

"Kricket..." he said after a few moments of silence. "Let me help you."

In response she sighed deeply and pulled away from him, silently debating her options. She honestly didn't have any, she realized. She'd entered a strange world where nothing made sense and where she was all alone. He'd offered to protect her. *Is that really such a bad thing*? she wondered to herself. He made it sound so easy, as if it was nothing more than an agreement between them, but life was never that simple, and people were rarely that nice. It had been a long time since someone had been kind and paid attention to her. Deciding she had no choice, she took the metal reader from him and glanced at it, although she had no idea what it said.

"Will you help me find my brothers?" she asked hopefully, giving him a decidedly child-like expression. Her eyes were red rimmed and puffy, not exactly pretty, but he found himself sympathizing with her nonetheless. There had been a time, not so long before, when he would have given anything to find his way home from his father's world and return to the life he'd known as a child.

"I promise to do my best to keep you safe," he returned definitively. "And I will help you, to the greatest of my ability, to navigate the sea in which you are now adrift."

"What do I have to do?" she asked, making her decision.

"Place your palm on the surface," he explained, handing her the reader. "It will register your handprint, which signifies that you are entering into the contract willingly and will abide by its terms."

"But I don't know its terms," she countered with a frown. "The symbols are strange; they don't make sense."

"Then you must take a leap of faith," he advised, far more calmly than he felt. At any moment, their meeting would be filed in the ship's log, and his father might be informed and change his mind. The captain might choose to seal the file, but he couldn't chance that information might spread back to his father before he was ready to confront him. Kricket technically didn't have a family patriarch in charge of her and was listed as an independent. That, however, would change if Cronus or her brothers claimed her before the contract was signed. It was a precarious position.

Slowly Kricket's eyes focused on the screen, then she placed her right palm against its surface and felt the warm glow of the scan that read and recorded her print. He smiled in relief—he couldn't help it—and she returned the smile shyly, uncertain what to do next.

"Now what?" she asked, but he simply shrugged and took the reader from her, closing the file and tossing it next to him on the long couch.

"That's all there is," he responded. For now at least, he added silently. It was an unusual situation, and he honestly wasn't sure what the next step should be. A short-term contract was not traditionally entered into by strangers, unless they had been caught in some sort of compromising situation. It was informal and vague and could be interpreted many different ways. There was, of course, the slight matter of consummation to make it completely and irrefutably binding, but even that definition was open to many interpretations. He supposed, technically, she had cried on his shoulder while he held her, alone in his private quarters, and that would be good enough for many. In any event, although he did, admittedly, find her extremely attractive, he had every intention of keeping his word and not making any unfitting demands in that category.

"We have different traditions," she said, twisting her hands together and giving him a tentative, lopsided grin.

"So I've heard," he mused, chuckling to himself. In the three months he'd spent in orbit, he and his cousin had indulged themselves a little too freely in the local customs—all in the name of collecting data on an unknown culture, of course.

"What have you heard?" she asked, curious and not sure how to take his remark.

CHAPTER TEN

"You kiss," he answered, thinking of his previous experiences and giving her a boyish grin that could only be described as wicked. His clandestine forays with his cousin had been particularly instructive in that regard. He would give her world one thing: they were masters of perverted physical seduction.

"So?" she returned. "What's wrong with that?"

He laughed out loud, a short burst followed by a warm and infectious chuckle that she found immensely appealing and very unlike the tense man she thought he was only an hour before.

"Nothing really. Not that I or anyone else would ever admit those sentiments publically," he confessed, eyes flickering mischievously in amusement and thinking the scribes and moderators would have had a field day with her comment, no matter how innocently it had been given. "It's not done. It's frowned upon in the most lenient societies, and, in many places, it's actually illegal."

"Why?" she asked, genuinely baffled. She liked it when he laughed, she decided. He didn't look nearly as old.

"Ahhh...well," he answered hesitantly, not quite sure how in depth of a conversation he wanted to have. He had discussed it at length with his cousin, but that was an entirely different situation. "It's considered...dirty."

"Why?" she pressed, her forehead knotted in confusion, but her eyes revealing that her amusement matched his. There were far dirtier things than kissing, she rationalized to herself. Not that she had experienced much more than the average make-out sessions of her peer group, but she wasn't an idiot. She knew what her friends and her brothers had to say about what came next.

"Because..." he hedged uneasily, stalling and trying to think of the right words. It was not a topic to be discussed openly unless there was a great deal of alcohol involved, and even then, never one he'd consider having with a female—even one he'd just signed a contract with. How could he possibly explain ten thousand years of germophobic segregation that had led to a plethora of strict and highly taboo social laws? "I suppose the easiest answer is because of the bacteria and viruses it spreads," he replied, faltering a bit over the words as a general sense of discomfort set in. Kissing, on the lips at least, was something a man usually had to pay a mistress to do and certainly something they never asked their wives for. "Humans are notorious for the microorganisms they harbor—the human bite is highly infectious. And because, if you're caught, it's basically...well, it's considered proof or confirmation—to the court at least—that other... things...things that under the law would require marriage...would have most likely occurred... even if the parties involved haven't signed the contracts yet," he stumbled, mentally chastising himself for not being able to speak about the subject intelligently.

"Oh..." she answered in an exaggerated tone, eyes twinkling mischievously. "So basically, if you're caught, you have to get married...and no one wants to get caught."

"In some respects...yes. But there are others who simply don't approve and find the general act of it repulsive," he admitted. "It's not talked about in polite society. It's more something you might participate in behind closed doors but never acknowledge for fear of being condemned as dirty or contaminated."

"Do you find it repulsive?" she asked curiously. The flirt in her was unable to resist, even though the more rational side of her was silently screaming at her to be cautious. Still, she found his discomfiture rather cute. Gone was the gruff, proud man who had questioned her earlier, and beside her sat someone far more relaxed, someone distinctly uncomfortable with the subject matter and yet almost playful and mischievous about it.

Subconsciously, she leaned forward, the tilt of her head and the expression in her eyes almost daring him to prove his position on the matter. *It wouldn't really be so bad to kiss him, would it?* she thought to herself, suddenly feeling slightly giddy and wondering where the thought had come from. She hadn't had the slightest interest in him before, but it had been a awfully long time since she'd been kissed, and much longer since she'd

CHAPTER TEN

been kissed by someone she was attracted to. *He's a handsome man*, her mind thought scandalously, somewhat shocking her. He'd been so nice to her, had held her when the tears got the better of her, had offered to protect her. Would it be so terribly wrong to see if, maybe, the contract she'd just agreed to offered a little more than just simple protection from the unknown?

Her action caught him off guard, and he wondered if William had been wrong about the strictness of her upbringing. There was no reason for it, and there was also equally no reason for the outrageous response it produced in him. It was if something unseen was deliberately pulling them together, but, even as he wondered at it, all logic and reasoning slipped from his mind.

Slowly he moved toward her until their bodies touched, and he lowered his head until his lips hovered just above hers, then paused, waiting to see her next reaction: if she shied away in retreat or welcomed his advance. She didn't move though, simply waited, unwittingly allowing the heat of anticipation to grow warm between them. There she remained, lips curled into a little smile, waiting patiently for him to prove his position.

"I think I've married a flirt," he muttered, and she giggled childishly, her smile curling wider and her head bobbing with the sound of it, causing her lips to just barely graze his.

It was enough. He utilized the movement to bring her mouth lightly into full contact with his. It was a unassuming kiss, nothing he would have considered particularly erotic, yet the energy that passed between them when their flesh met was utterly intoxicating, and he lingered far longer than he'd intended. When she didn't resist, he deepened it further, arms pulling her closer toward him.

Kricket wondered briefly what she thought she was doing, then dismissed the thought and gave in to the moment. She wasn't acting at all like herself, and, worse, she didn't care. She sighed contentedly as he wrapped his arms around her, understanding that she had very little time to call things to a halt, but, at the same time, not really wanting to. He was a wonderful kisser, she was enjoying the feeling of being held, and she wanted desperately to believe in the fairy tale emotion of the moment—even if she knew that reality would probably shatter it later. It was only when his hands trailed up her back to her neck, unconsciously pulling her roughly closer to him in an effort to intensify the growing intimacy, that she yelped in pain and realized what she was doing.

"Are you all right?" he asked breathlessly, stunned by the intimacy that had erupted so spontaneously between them.

"My neck," she cried, hands coming up protectively to cover the light bruises that still lingered there. Her neck had been stiff when she left the medical bay, but it hadn't hurt until he'd touched it. As the unexpected pain shot up and down her spine, tears formed rebelliously in her eyes again.

"Should I send for Dr. Xnam?" he asked, mortified that he might have inadvertently harmed her. The girl was barely an hour out of the medical bay, and he'd pounced on her like an unrestrained idiot. He hadn't been thinking; he'd merely reacted.

"No," she answered, although, by the look on her face, he was less than assured. "It's fine, really. I don't want to go back there. She'll just lock me up and pack me in ice again."

He regarded her quietly for several long seconds, until her eyes shyly found their way back to his. "Are you sure?" he asked, resisting the urge to take her back, despite her protests.

"I'm fine," she answered quietly, and he nodded in acquiescence.

"Come here," He said gently, reaching out and pulling her back into his arms. To his delight, she returned easily into his embrace and settled close to him, her head gently tucked back against his shoulder.

"I'm thinking, perhaps..." he offered cautiously, "this alliance of ours might turn out to be a good thing."

To his enchantment, she giggled.

***

The goddess Ilearia watched silently from beyond the image

CHAPTER TEN

of the garden as the girl settled quietly into Coltame's embrace, somewhat irritated that the physical pain of her injury had broken the spell between them. She needed the two bonded together; too much time had already been wasted. Lifting her hand gently, she waved ethereal fingers and watched as both fell into a deep sleep, then gently reinforced his sense of duty, his need to assure the girl's safety and protection. It wasn't ideal, but it would have to do.

"You promised," her husband's voice echoed, gently reprimanding her.

"I need them together," she answered, sheepish over having been caught interfering, yet unwilling to repent for her meddling.

"You promised to allow them to choose for themselves," Irage reprimanded. "If you interfere, we run the risk that it won't last, and they'll only resent it later. Let them come together on their own, choose for themselves. That is the only bond that will endure, and you know it."

"They're taking too much time," she pronounced, closing the window on the mortal plane and pulling them both safely beyond the gates of their own dimension. "Zoujin is dying; the Uhnman are making their move."

"She is my responsibility, Ilearia, not yours," he reminded her firmly as she walked past him, up the garden path to their home. "This is my assignment, my mission."

"Of course, darling," she crooned gently, though he had no doubts she was not only unrepentant but would continue to interfere.

***

"Goman?" Ceya asked incredulously, lowering herself slowly into a small seat across from the desk in her brother's private office. "Here? In person?"

"That means the emperor knew, and he's now moving to protect his interest," Jaget replied. "I need to know what Rastmus has told you," he said pointedly, and then, at her startled remonstration, added, "My dear, I may be the captain of this vessel, but I am also your devoted older brother and the patriarch of our line. The two of you can pretend to the rest of the universe that your alliance with Rastmus ended with Coltame's birth, but do not presume that I am unaware that it did not. You still communicate with him via private transmissions and, I suspect, have rendezvoused with him secretly on more than one occasion."

Ceya paused and regarded her brother cautiously for several long seconds before exhaling sharply and turning her head to the wall. She was not a young girl anymore, but a woman who had done her duty to her family and her empire by marrying well the first time out and producing a son.

"I'm not threatening you, Ceya," he offered kindly. "If anything, I sympathize, which is why I've kept this knowledge to myself and prevented others from commenting on it, but Rastmus isn't a boy anymore. He's grown into a very powerful man. Many say he's the emperor's first choice to succeed. I need to know why Goman himself is coming to see the girl. I need to know if he's given you some insight that I'm not privy to."

"He's said nothing," she replied honestly, and he sank back into his chair in frustration.

"Gage was on duty last night when the Professor tried to abduct the girl and take her to Malizore," he began in an exasperated tone, born of his own frustrations. "His interview with her revealed that Hollin might have fled to this planet with the Princess Meera. It was also discussed that the girl could, possibly, be the biological progeny of Senator Cronus via Hollin and Meera's daughter. Medical is confirming these suspicions now."

Ceya couldn't help the exclamation that crossed her lips as she cursed in frustration. The Delsheni Senator was a distant cousin of her mother, and had been the bane of her existence for her entire life. "He knew then," she stated coldly. "He's known all along where Hollin was."

"He's apparently produced four sons with the daughter, in

CHAPTER TEN

addition to the girl we're harboring," Jaget revealed evenly, smiling wearily at her look of outraged astonishment. "Gage is young and idealistic. He believes Cronus intended five sons to pilot the five crafts that form Hollin's robot, and, knowing Cronus as I do, I can't discount that theory," he added with a foreboding chuckle. "But of more importance, four grandsons of *Princess Meera*—four grown sons of Meera's line. He's going to make a play for the throne when the emperor dies."

"War," she breathed softly. "He's going to push through the Delsheni secession from the empire and put humanity at war with each other again, even though there's far too precious few of us to fight each other, and the Roan, and the Trogoul all at once."

"I suspect he's desperate," Jaget mused out loud, hand absently reaching to scratch at his goatee in an unconscious gesture. "He's now old and past his prime. Rastmus is young; he could rule for decades. Rastmus is also a good candidate, appreciated by both powers and better regarded than any of Cronus's official offspring. He's half Delsheni; his son is three quarters Delsheni. There are many who would support that transition over Cronus or his heirs. But these new boys, if it can be proved they're Meera's descendants through Hollin…"

"Neither Rastmus or Coltame are his pawns," she spat, unable to keep the bitterness out of her voice. "They've embraced their Rheigan heritage. Despite their genes, they're not Delsheni enough to bow to his will," she added, and her brother merely nodded solemnly in agreement.

"Now Goman himself is coming to inspect the girl," he replied thoughtfully. "He must have left the capital the moment the news broke, on the emperor's fastest ship, to arrive so quickly. My guess is he'll snatch her back to Syphlein as quickly as possible."

"Why?" Ceya asked, using her fingertips to rub at the stress aching in her temples. It was far too early in the morning to be once again thrust into one of the old senator's schemes. "She's female; the matriarchies are solid and no real threat."

"Her overnight celebrity is mind-boggling," her brother returned. "In the five days since she wounded Malizore, that's all that the news channels are buzzing about. If I were them, I'd be very concerned. They'll likely play her into their propaganda somehow. They can't allow her to be shuttled off to Aelis where she can be used as a sounding post to reinstate Azill's line. Gage said that Coltame informed him last night that he was to be given the girl for one year. I doubt he's their first choice, more like the most convenient. They'll secure her for themselves, out of Cronus's reach, and prep her for a more advantageous marriage within the hierarchy; you watch."

"But why?" she asked in surprise. She had seen with her own eyes that her son was legitimately interested in the girl, but she also knew that his father needed an alliance with Horshell to ensure his succession. His daughter and Coltame were already betrothed. One year wouldn't postpone things much, but the emperor was ill. If he died before the alliance was made, Horshell might back his own nephews over Rastmus.

"I believe..." he began, then stopped as a chirping sound notified him of an incoming transmission. Scanning it via the reader embedded in his desk, his eyebrows rose.

"What is it?" she asked curiously.

"It appears Senator Cronus is less than an hour away from rendezvousing with us," he answered slowly, eyes rescanning the details of the transmission. "We are to hold our position and receive his shuttle...And I am ordered to clear my schedule to receive him immediately upon docking."

Ceya snorted in disgust, teeth grinding against one another. They were in orbit around the planet's moon and had been for several months. It wasn't likely the old senator was in any danger of them breaking free and running for it; although she, personally, was tempted to. "Arrogant of him," she replied. "You're supposed to clear your schedule? This is your ship. He's not on Aelis. You're the reigning power here, not him."

"I'm curious as to what he has to say," Jaget countered absently, tapping a silent reply into the computer screen. "I'm

CHAPTER TEN

stunned how quickly both managed to get to us. The fuss this girl is causing reveals more is going on here than meets the eye."

"What did you say in your response?" she asked curiously.

"That Goman's ship docks within three hours, and I will receive them both simultaneously, not before." He paused and regarded his sister meaningfully, silently wishing he could be present when the head of their mother's family realized the emperor's vizier had also journeyed at top speed and nearly beaten him the punch. "And I've also just been informed that, just before the standard dawn this morning, your son filed documentation legitimizing a contract between himself and the girl, which was apparently written by Rastmus himself."

***

Coltame jerked awake with the first chime, stunned he'd actually fallen asleep. Sprawled across him on the couch, the girl stirred at his movement but didn't wake.

A second chime sounded, and his hand quickly let go of his hold on her to search out the reader, which had fallen back into the cushions. This time, however, her eyes fluttered open, and she sat up groggily, blinking hard in an effort to remember where she was. Cursing, he pried the reader out from under them and acknowledged the chime, only to have a screen full of messages assault his eyes.

"What was that noise?" she asked sleepily, watching as the lights of the board illuminated his face in the darkened room. She'd been deeply asleep, dreaming about her brothers, about the simple days before the invaders came, and it was strange to wake up to a entirely different reality where life was uncertain and scary again.

"My secretary sending me my agenda," he replied absently. "The morning shift has begun, and I'm afraid I've slept through several of my first appointments."

"That's not good," she responded, hand tentatively patting down her hair in case it was as tangled as she feared it was.

He seemed not to notice her comment though, his attention absorbed in the contents of the screen. She sat up a little straighter, awkwardly pulling her clothing back into some semblance of order and trying to shake the sleep from her mind. She'd never fallen asleep with someone before, and she wasn't sure exactly what she was expected to do afterward; so she simply sat quietly and watched him.

After several long minutes, he switched the reader off and tossed it on the floor above the sunken couch. "It was apparently an interesting night," he commented, the hard tone she remembered earlier slipping back into his voice. "Dr. Xnam has confirmed Cronus as your biological father. Malizore's camp is demanding two of his most notorious generals and you in return for your mother, and the captain has sent a message that both Cronus and Goman, the emperor's most trusted adviser, will arrive within the hour."

"My mother's still alive?" she asked, eyes bright with hope, hardly hearing anything else he had said.

"Yes, apparently negotiations have begun," he assured her. "Malizore now knows who he has, and we know who he has; things should proceed civilly enough for now. In the meantime, I'm to take you immediately back to Dr. Xnam for another physical and then to the captain's conference room, where they will decide if the contract we signed is legal and who has the best claim on you."

"But I thought the contract meant…" she began, but didn't finish. Wasn't the whole point of signing the contract that she would stay with him?

"Cronus is the patriarch of a very large and very powerful Delsheni family—one that my mother and the captain both descend from. You're not a formally recognized daughter, so he's at a disadvantage. But he could claim that he had future plans to recognize you and that he should be the one who decides where you go. I have no idea why Goman himself would travel to the edges of the galaxy, but hopefully he's here to argue in my favor and not confiscate you for the empire."

CHAPTER TEN

"Recognize me?" she asked, trying hard to follow what he was saying, but not actually succeeding.

"By law, claims to biological parentage have little weight," he explained. "Just because you are Cronus's natural offspring does not give him authority over you or you the right to claim membership in his family line. He can, if he chooses, officially recognize you now, but we've already signed a contract that designates me as your legal spokesman. A contract that he's currently demanding be nullified."

"The Professor said Cronus took my brothers when the Roan invaded, but he didn't want me. Why would he come for me now?"

"Because you're famous now," he said acerbically. "Your stabbing of Malizore not only maimed him, it emasculated him. For the first time since Braun nearly blew his head off two decades ago, he's wounded and weak. That's seen as an incredibly heroic act. That it was accomplished by Hollin's granddaughter, the man who saved humanity from the Trogoul...Let's just say people are very excited about your return to society."

"So when I was disposable, he left me to die, but now that I'm famous, he's decided maybe he wants me after all," she concluded resentfully.

"That and your genetic charts are going to expose he not only knew where Hollin was and didn't say anything, which was treason, but it's going to come out that he kept your mother as a mistress and impregnated her seven times without the courtesy of a contract. Worse, seven pregnancies on one female screams of abusive medical intervention, possibly even artificial birthing tanks, which is taboo in the most lenient societies and completely illegal among the mainstream worlds of the empire. Humans spent way too many years splicing genes and cloning; it nearly destroyed us. The current laws and popular opinion now strongly frown upon it. No, left unchecked, my guess is that the outrage of the public, and the slander that will be thrown against his household for defiling the daughter of a legendary hero in such an offensive manner, is going to make the emperor's legalization of concubine harems for the Rheigan royals look mundane."

"So I'm an embarrassment," she summarized. "He has to publically make nice with me so no one catches him being the ass he is and holds him accountable."

Coltame regarded her for several long seconds, watching the anger in her eyes ignite and smolder. She was a tough little thing—he'd give her that. He wasn't sure he'd have held up nearly as well if the situation was reversed. Senator Cronus didn't scare him, but he could, possibly, make life difficult for him—especially regarding Kricket. He was fairly certain though that he could navigate whatever hazards the conniving old man threw his way, but Goman, on the other hand, concerned him greatly. There was no reason for the ancient vizier to journey this far out into nowhere so quickly, which meant there was another plan in play that he knew nothing about. A man's greatest enemy was the plot he didn't see coming.

"I want nothing to do with my so-called father," she said, recalcitrant. "He never bothered to see us, he took my brothers and left me for dead, then tried to give me to Malizore in exchange for my mother...Isn't that the same as trying to kill me? How do I know he isn't going to turn around and offer me back up like he did before? Can't you tell him to leave me alone?"

"Unfortunately the contract isn't a full day old yet. Your father, recognized or not, is challenging its legitimacy," he responded dryly.

"How can he do that?" she asked, bile rising. She liked the man in front of her or, at the very least, liked the way he kissed, which she supposed was better than nothing. At any rate, she'd rather stay with him than go off with a man who'd tried to trade her life away without ever meeting her. If it didn't work, she'd be free in a year; she could live with that. Who knew what would happen if this unknown person came barreling back into her life.

CHAPTER TEN

"Because there was no provision for a bride price to be paid at the contract's end, which means you wouldn't be compensated with money, lands, or a title. Therefore I would basically be able to walk away from it and leave you stranded, which I would never be so dishonorable to do. He's also claiming we haven't had time to consummate it and make it binding. In the meantime, I've been ordered, on my honor as my father's son, not to touch you until the status of our alliance is determined."

"But you said all it took was a kiss..." she offered hesitantly.

"Yes, and that's what I'm going to argue, as delicately as possible. You were alone with me in my private quarters when the contract was signed, we were physically intimate, and we slept together in close proximity. I don't see how he can negate it. Even if he did, what happened between us last night would be transgression enough to demand a second contract to be renegotiated."

"So we're okay?" she asked uncertainly. She felt as if the rug had been pulled out from under her again. A few hours before, life seemed to be settling down, but now she was just as full of anxiety as she'd been in the medical bay.

Coltame was silent for a few moments, weighing his options, his eyes dark and calculating. "We should be fine," he answered. "But Goman's appearance bothers me. He's unbelievably old and one of the most influential men at court. There's no reason for him to travel all this way, and I'm not sure what his presence at the table means."

"So now what?" she asked uncertainly.

He regarded her frankly for a few moments and then replied, "Now we fight."

11

CHAPTER ELEVEN

Kricket sat in the small waiting room—for what seemed like forever—then stood and paced for another eternity. She could have been confined to the room for an hour or six hours; there was no way to tell. She was frustrated, anxious, and felt at any moment that the strange, bland, gelatinous breakfast she'd been fed was going to be regurgitated all over the floor in front of her.

With little ceremony, Coltame had reluctantly taken her back to the medical bay, where Dr. Xnam and another physician she didn't know had performed an extremely tedious and careful examination, which had left her even more distressed and fretful than before. She'd then been fed an unappetizing mound of protein and vitamins that Xnam assured her was good for her. Finally she was given a standard, civilian uniform, then escorted to the waiting room. Between the weird food, the strange clothes, the unfamiliar room, and the bizarre situation she found herself in, she thought she might go insane if someone didn't immediately open the door and explain what was happening in the room beyond.

As if in response to some unknown, silent, command by her

CHAPTER ELVEN

thoughts, the doorway slid open, and a young officer motioned her forward. She surprised herself by hesitating, unsure and a bit frightened now that the time had come for her to actually do something. If her grandfather had been there, he would have barked at her to pull her shoulders back and get her chin high off the ground. He would say that there was only one way to solve a problem, and that was to deal with it head-on, not hide in the closet and hope it went away. As she thought of him, she felt again the warm glow that was always there when she was sick or hurt or frightened. The feeling reminded her of him, reassuring her, and, almost unconsciously, the nervousness fluttered away, and the soft gray of her eyes hardened into the steel that had seen her through the toughest times of the past few years.

The room inside was not much larger than the waiting room and seemed dominated by a long, narrow, tiered table. At one end, slightly raised from the rest of the assembled crowd, was an older man whom she assumed was the captain of the ship. Of more importance to her though, directly in front of her, on the far side of the table, sat all four of her brothers.

She couldn't help the smile of pure joy that escaped her. She was still furious with them for abandoning her, but there they were, alive and well, and all the grief and guilt and anguish she'd experienced upon their deaths catapulted into the sheer elation and the relief of seeing them once again in front of her. Without thinking, she rushed forward and was met halfway in a gigantic bear hug by her next oldest brother, Steven, crying out his name in a near sob of joy. She turned and would have offered the same greeting to the other three, but the expressions she met with were far from welcoming. If anything, the disapproval dripping from their faces was enough to stop her cold and make Steven shuffle uncomfortably, retaking his seat without looking at her.

"You will restrain yourself, Kirsten," her eldest brother, George, growled contemptuously. He'd grown even rounder than the last time she'd seen him, surpassing even his self-described "hefty" and ballooning into full-fledged obesity.

"Your actions, as usual, are highly inappropriate, considering the circumstances."

"Considering you're supposed to be dead?" she snapped, falling easily back into the prickly way she'd learned to handle an overbearing sibling, someone who considered himself some sort of self-styled imperator to be obeyed. "Oh yes, I forgot. You abandoned me and saved your own asses at the expense of mine," she added waspishly, causing several eyebrows in the room to rise in surprise. There were eleven years between them, so he'd been almost grown and off to college by the time she seriously began to express herself, never having to deal with him for more than just holiday visits. While the others would automatically defer to him, mostly to avoid the inevitable pounding they'd get if they refused, she'd always stubbornly defied him.

"Sit down, Kirsten," he reprimanded in return, but she was unfazed, and it showed in her impertinent body language.

Her chin lifted haughtily, and her shoulders threw themselves backward as if readying herself for a confrontation. For the first time, she regarded her brothers through the critical eye of a sibling who'd been wronged. They'd abandoned her and left her for dead, then their professed father had tried to barter her back to a man who wanted to kill her; she needed to remember that.

They looked well fed, which showed they hadn't had to endure the strict rations and near starvation she had. They were no longer dressed in the jeans and casual shirts she knew them to favor, but in supremely elegant and courtly clothes that were far more reminiscent of other times. Although the pants were long and similar to what she might have seen on her own world, the shirt-jackets worn over them were heavily brocaded and flared from the waist, resting halfway up their thighs. On each shoulder was attached a heavy metallic clip littered with sparkling gemstones, which held the ends to equally heavy and expensive-looking capes. They looked like ridiculous, overstuffed peacocks.

"Nice to see you too, George," she responded, her words

CHAPTER ELVEN

dripping with acid. "Very pretty clothes. Tell me, does the silk on your chest extend to your pretty little panties as well?"

"How dare you—" her eldest brother roared.

"People are starving back home," she countered frostily, cutting him off. "Our neighbors, our friends, Mom, and I. People are disappearing and dying horrible deaths, and you're dressed up like a fattened pig pretending to be—"

"Kricket Holland," Jaget interrupted in an even tone. He wasn't sure what he had expected the girl to be, but after several hours of deliberation with her insipid brothers, it wasn't the brazen little female in front of him. She was absurdly tiny, much smaller than he'd anticipated, yet she showed absolutely no signs of being intimidated by any of the prominent men assembled to determine her fate. Her brothers had proven to be as vain and arrogant as their sire, but the girl seemed to take none of it. In fact, she chastised them as efficiently and thoroughly as if she were the eldest son instead of the youngest daughter. "Is that the name you're known by?" he added mildly.

"Her name is Kirsten," George snapped, returning to his seat even though his cheeks had reddened with anger and his breath quickened. "Kricket is a senseless nickname given to her as a joke when she was five."

"You can call me whatever you want, George," she responded, crossing her arms in front of her, eyes defiant. A small, wicked grin creased the sides of her mouth, revealing she enjoyed baiting him. "Whether I'll answer or not is another matter."

With that, her eldest brother jumped to his feet again, while all three of his younger male siblings seemed to sink lower in their chairs. His face turned beet red, and he began to sweat; his puffy fists balled up as if he was ready to attack her. In response, her arms uncrossed, and she shifted into a loose and ready position, as if challenging him to make good on his silent threat.

Eyes darting from the large and overweight eldest son to the petite, half-starved hellion of a youngest daughter, Jaget watched the scene unfold with a feeling that was a cross between hilarity and annoyance. He admired the girl for her spiritedness, but, realizing this was not the time or place for siblings to air their disagreements, he intervened by holding up his hand for them to stop. "Please be seated, young lady," he ordered in a calm but stern voice. "Kricket is the name on the contract, and, by everyone's agreement, despite the differences in planetary versus standard calendars, she is old enough to at least decide on her name."

Kricket gave George a triumphant look as she seated herself in the only chair left at the table, directly at the opposite end from the captain. To her amusement, her eldest brother glowered but seated himself and remained silent. It was only then that she began to genuinely look at the others present.

The man she assumed to be the captain of the ship was dressed in what anyone could recognize as a full ceremonial uniform. He was old enough to have gray hair, but not nearly as old as the two men on either side of him, each one step down from the three-tiered table.

There was no mistaking the man on his left. He looked exactly like an older version of her brothers. The disdainful way Cronus regarded her left her no doubt that the Professor had been honest when said that her father hadn't wanted her. He was richly dressed, far better than any of the others in the room, but the splendor of the clothes did nothing to hide the arrogance and pugnaciousness of the face any more than the fading good looks could hide the coldness of his eyes. George and her brothers were seated on the lowest tier, oldest to youngest, all of them looking distinctly uncomfortable and refusing to meet her eyes.

Turning her gaze in the other direction, she turned to look at the man on the opposite side of the captain. He was ancient beyond words, yet his calm and serene eyes held nothing but strength and a vitality of spirit that belied the paper-thin skin and gnarled fingers. He was dressed every bit as richly as those on the opposite side of the long table, but his silks were plain, devoid of brocade, and he wore no gemstones or embellishments. It was a study in contrasts, and, at first glance,

CHAPTER ELVEN

she liked him for it, if for no other reason. But as his wizened blue eyes leveled stoically on hers, she had the distinct and irrevocable impression of a kindred spirit, and she liked him for that even more.

Seated to his right, she was surprised to see Coltame, who she barely recognized in his dress clothes of dark green and gold. Like the older man next to him, he wore very little embellishment on the fabric, but there was no mistaking his rank. His hair was pulled back from his face and tied at the neck with a thick gold cord. His look was dark and foreboding, and significantly different from the impish young man who'd kissed and cuddled her the night before. He didn't return her gaze. Instead his eyes scanned the reader in front of him intently, as if he were bored and the proceedings were intruding on far more serious work. The snub pricked at her, and she wondered if she'd been mistaken to think there'd been a budding closeness between them. For the first time, she realized that he was, indeed, an extremely important person and that she had very little significance at all.

Self-consciously she pulled at the plain, unflattering, standard clothing she'd been given. It was a sturdy two-piece jumpsuit and tolerably comfortable, but she didn't think it suited her small frame any more than the dye of the drab fabric suited her hair and skin tone. The top was very modest, with a high collar, long sleeves, and a stiff, full skirt that descended about halfway down her calf. The whole thing made her feel like a preschooler in an old-fashioned skating costume that was far too large for her.

Shifting her attention back to the others in the room, she noticed a woman sitting next to Coltame who was probably twenty-five or thirty years older than she was. She was dressed in a military ensemble that wasn't quite as elaborate as the captain's, but very close. The woman gave her a warm, pleasant smile, and she felt her own lips curl slightly upward in return.

Next to her was another man she didn't know. He was middle-aged, dressed well, and, like Coltame, paid more attention to the reader in front of him than to the proceedings.

"Do you know why you're here?" the captain asked plainly, bringing her attention back to him.

"I suspect it has something to do with the contract I signed last night," she returned in a similar tone.

"We are here to make sure you understand your options," the ancient man next to the captain supplied in a surprisingly strong voice, his eyes twinkling as if he knew a secret she didn't.

"Then shouldn't you have consulted me before deliberating them behind my back?" she asked bluntly, slightly surprised by the sharp intake of breath around her. Even Coltame's head snapped up to regard her in amazement, eyes shifting to cautiously glance at the man next to him.

Goman, however, simply appeared amused. The girl was the striking, and almost terrifying, physical embodiment of her grandmother, but the way she'd publically dressed down her eldest brother was her grandfather incarnate. The comparison tickled him. How Hollin must have grieved the banality of his grandsons, but the granddaughter…The granddaughter was likely to prove her grandsire's last laugh on the universe—especially if he had anything to do with it. With a sudden aching in his chest, he realized just how much he wished Hollin was there to share the thought with and just how much he had missed his old friend.

"We have concluded that, perhaps, you may have not been presented with all the alternatives you might have otherwise been offered before signing," Jaget explained. "Unfortunately, given the uniqueness of the situation, we weren't even sure what those options were until after we'd deliberated them. Senator Cronus has offered to formally recognize you, just as he has recognized your brothers."

"How kind of him," she droned in return, obviously unimpressed by the honor. "Perhaps he would like to explain why he's suddenly changed his mind? I mean, last I heard, I was an expendable bone to be thrown back at Malizore."

"Young lady, you need to understand that what the senator is offering is a great honor," Jaget returned coldly, eyes shifting

CHAPTER ELVEN

from kind arbitrator back into those of a captain who was used to authority and respect. "He is a very powerful man who can educate you and find a very good marriage alliance for you."

"You don't consider a marriage to Coltame a good alliance?" she volleyed, unfazed. She wasn't sure what kind of reaction she'd get, but it was obvious she'd surprised them. The captain's eyes widened slightly, and there was a great deal of shuffling on both sides of the table.

"That's not what we intended to insinuate," he clarified. The last thing he needed was for Coltame to cry insult at the eleventh hour. Tempers had finally cooled, and both sides were willing to stand down long enough to hear the girl's opinion. Until that point, Coltame had taken a slightly contrite but firm stance that he might, perhaps, have been mistaken to push things through so quickly but that he had acted in the interests of the empire before the girl's parentage had been firmly established. However, if his nephew suddenly changed tactics and claimed Cronus dishonored him by suggesting the match was not good enough for his unrecognized daughter, Rastmus would charge to defend his son's wounded honor, and the whole argument might be blown out of proportion again. "The contract you signed is a one-year term without any provisions for you at its end," he explained, reiterating the final consensus that they had deliberated. "The simple facts of the matter are, you are forfeiting your potential marketability for a stronger, long-term alliance later on and not receiving any form of substantial compensation. You'll be right back in a similar situation to the one you are in now, but with no one to provide for you."

"But if I understand correctly," she answered, with far more maturity than he would have previously given her credit for, "during this one year, I'm also offered food, shelter, and protection from Malizore—as well as an opportunity to study and learn about the society I'm now forced to live in."

"Yes," he answered simply. "That is correct."

"Then I have all I need," she replied. "I have a year to learn how to provide for myself. If things work out, great, we can continue. If they don't, then I can survive just fine on my own."

"This is outrageous!" the man she assumed was her father declared, breaking his silence. "I have never, in the history of deliberating—"

"Senator, please," Jaget interrupted, giving the man a hard look. "Now is the time for the girl to speak. We can consider her wishes in conjunction with the law afterward. Until that time, no one will speak unless I have given them leave to." Turning to Kricket, he took a deep breath, calmed himself, and added, "Young lady, you do not seem to understand. In one year, you will not have the option to renew. His Highness has already been contracted into a long-term alliance that will take effect upon the completion of the short term. When your current contract dissolves, you will not have a husband, and you will not have a patriarch to negotiate another for you."

Cautiously her eyes shifted in Coltame's direction. It hadn't occurred to her that he might already have another relationship with someone else; it burned. He'd kissed her, cuddled her, let her cry on his shoulder, and all the time he'd known there was someone else waiting for him. *If that wasn't a man for you*, she thought bitterly to herself. "I do not need, nor have I ever needed, a man to speak for me," she returned coldly, surprising everyone present.

"Young lady..."

"I'll be fine," she interrupted in a firm, commanding voice that belied her tiny stature. "I have a one-year cushion in which to learn the survival skills I need, and after that..." She paused and thought about the unknown. "Have you ever had your world destroyed?" she asked frankly.

In response, he sat back, taken off guard by her words and not sure how to answer. He had lived through the destruction of his world as a child, lived through the horrors of being defeated by the Trogoul. He understood, but now was not the time or place to communicate his commiseration.

"My whole world came crashing down about a year ago," she continued without waiting for his answer. "While my brothers

CHAPTER ELVEN

hauled ass at the first sign of trouble, I was left behind to starve in the shelters. I not only survived, I kept my mom and William alive too. Being left stranded in a hopeless situation isn't anything new, and it's nothing I can't handle."

"I've had enough of this," Cronus spat. "The physicians have presented evidence that the marriage was not physically consummated by traditional means. I am willing to recognize the girl—"

"I have a name," Kricket nearly snarled, eyes cold as she leveled them against the man she knew was her father but who hadn't even bothered to introduce himself when he finally came face to face with her. The man who had taken her brothers but not her; the man who would have given her back to Malizore.

"I beg your pardon?" he returned indignantly, turning hard, angry eyes on the little hellion he'd spawned. She had no right to speak to him unless he gave her permission to. She was nothing, an unauthorized mistake—a costly one at that.

"I have a name," she repeated in an impertinent tone. "Or have you even bothered to learn it?"

"You insolent little…" her eldest brother blustered, standing and pushing his chair back as if to move in her direction.

"Oh shut up, George," she almost shouted in response, also pushing her chair back and standing in case he actually moved. It wouldn't be the first time he'd physically gone after her, and it wouldn't be the last that she'd give as good as she got. He might have once been able to get the better of her, but over the last year, while he'd been growing fat and lazy, she'd been learning street fighting and how to survive.

"You want to fight me?" she snarled. "Then get over here and bring it on. You're nothing but a fat coward and always were. You, I could understand, but the rest of you?" she asked, turning her gaze one by one on her three other brothers. "You should be ashamed of yourselves. The second things got a little dicey you bailed and left Mom and me to face the invaders on our own. Da, our grandfather, would have been so proud of the way you rushed to save your own skins first," she added sarcastically, and at least Steven had the decency to hang his head. "Well, go back to whatever rock you've been hiding under; I don't want you. Enjoy your pretty clothes and snug beds. I'm going to stay here and focus on stopping Malizore and freeing our world."

"Kricket," Jaget interrupted. He hadn't shouted, but the authority in his voice was enough to silence her and draw her attention. "Please sit down," he commanded in a firm, no-nonsense tone, and she silently did so. "Senator," he added coldly, "if you or your son interrupt again, I will have all of you removed from these proceedings."

An awkward silence descended upon the room, tensions high as Kricket and the left-hand side of the table retreated to stewing quietly in their own anger. Jaget allowed it to continue for several long seconds, carefully observing the reactions of all present.

Senator Cronus, who hadn't anticipated resistance to his claims, was uncharacteristically agitated and arguing his rights far more tenaciously than could have been predicted. In any normal circumstance, he should be expected to back down and renounce his claims, letting the contract stand with a few basic modifications. Jaget was surprised to find the girl was not a modest and shy Delsheni maiden. In fact, she was proving to be quite the opposite. Why Cronus was arguing so tenaciously over a daughter he'd never met, and who obviously didn't want his aid, made Jaget wonder just what the senator had to lose with the girl not securely under his control. Coltame, for his part, while presenting a fairly convincing front that he was far too busy with other matters and didn't particularly care what outcome was decided, was also arguing far too doggedly for his ambivalence to be credible.

"Now that I have everyone's attention," Jaget said, words and body language exuding his authority on the ship, "we will continue this hearing in a civilized manner." Turning to Kricket, he added, "Young lady, I am fully prepared to rule that you are of sound mind and competent to accept this contract. However, I'm less than assured that you understand what it is you've

CHAPTER ELVEN

gotten yourself into and what you are giving up. Senator Cronus has agreed to formally recognize you as his daughter, to give you a legal family, a link to a very desirable heritage that you will never be able to replace."

"He may recognize me," she replied evenly, eyes hard. "But I do not recognize him."

"I beg your pardon?" Jaget replied as the room, as one, stared at her in astonishment. No one ever turned down formal recognition, especially to such a prestigious line. Recognition was the most sought-after designation in their society.

"I do not recognize him," she repeated coldly. There was no way she would ever align herself with the arrogant man glaring at her now as if he could mentally strangle her. He had taken her brothers and left her behind on a broken world to die, then told the Professor to give her to Malizore—proof she meant nothing to him.

"Kricket," Ceya spoke up gently, drawing her attention, "in our society, formal recognition is nearly everything. It defines who you are, what line you descend from, what social circles you may associate with. You have a chance to be associated with a very powerful Delsheni royal house. Be very careful you don't regret hasty words later on."

"I'm Margaret Holland's daughter, George Holland's granddaughter," she answered, chin high. "That's the only association I need."

"I've heard enough," Cronus said harshly. "The girl is obviously ignorant and can be excused her lack of manners. She is barely past her majority, too young to breed, and no one here can seriously argue that she in any way understands the choices she is making. I want her released from that damnable contract and into my custody immediately."

"Did your grandfather ever recognize you?" Coltame asked curiously. He was shocked by Kricket's behavior. She'd been openly joyful to see her brothers, and he'd been terrified she might change her mind and accept their offer to take her home with them. It had been almost genius of Cronus to bring them. A young girl in her situation would have been justifiably expected to have run to them, but she'd harshly chastised them instead, openly exposing to a formal court her indignation over their abandonment of her.

The newfound grandsons of Hollin didn't impress Coltame much. They were in lockstep with the oldest and, in the hours they'd spent arguing Kricket's fate before she had been brought in, hadn't deviated once from what seemed to him a well-rehearsed script. The second oldest son was smart, had argued intelligently and effectively, and might develop into a force to be reckoned with someday, but the eldest was a puffed-up copy of his sire, and the youngest, the one Kricket had named Steven, obviously a brow-beaten weakling. Kricket's claim that she was her mother's daughter, her grandfather's granddaughter, intrigued him. Hollin had never formally recognized any children, but he'd never had the opportunity to. Cronus was arguing he had written proof that Hollin intended to recognize his grandsons whenever the possibility presented itself, which was precarious at best, but might just hold up. If he had somehow recognized his granddaughter in the same fashion, then perhaps she wasn't a free agent after all, but Hollin's orphan. It was interesting to ponder anyway.

"How could he?" Cronus blustered back. "There's no formal court on that world."

"It doesn't matter," Coltame argued. "If you can argue that Giagous Hollin intended to recognized his blood grandsons by calling them his grandsons in front of the colonists, many of whom are intergalactic citizens and can provide testimony, then the same could be construed for the girl. If he called her his granddaughter, if she called him grandfather, then her line should technically descend from there. Da means father in older Rheigan writings; it's still used today in some dialects. If that was what she called him, if that was what he allowed himself to be publically called—"

"You're mincing words," Cronus interrupted. "I have correspondence, in Hollin's own voice and legal seal,

CHAPTER ELVEN

acknowledging my sons as his descendants."

"And the daughter?" Goman asked pointedly. "Does that correspondence recognize the daughter? The extreme swiftness of your arrival and the persistence of your arguments seem to suggest, perhaps, you have more information than we are currently aware of."

Cronus shifted uncomfortably in his seat. To any other court he might be able to get away with saying no, but Goman was present, and the damn vizier could see through any deception or front he might provide. Hollin had been extremely careful to mention the girl in almost every reference of his family since her birth, virtually assuring she'd have to be recognized along with them. If she had died or been lost in the shuffle of the invasion, it wouldn't have been a problem. But now that she was very much in the public eye, he had almost no choice but to acknowledge her as well. "Yes," he answered tersely.

"There we have it then," Goman replied sanguinely. "She refuses her connections to the senator, which she has the legal right to, and claims her connections to her grandfather's line. As the senator has so graciously testified, Hollin acknowledged the girl in formal correspondence and publically before citizens of the empire who can bear testimony. It is, I believe, enough."

The man Kricket didn't know spoke up. "Are you saying you would be willing to endorse the claims that Hollin's will was to recognize his grandsons as his own?"

"I am saying, Ambassador Morwin," Goman continued in a gentle voice that still managed to resound throughout the meeting room, "that the senator has provided testimony that Hollin demonstrated, to the best of his ability and on more than one occasion, his intentions toward his daughter and her children, given the unavailability of a formal court with which to certify them. He acknowledged all his grandchildren both publically and in formal documents; we must accept all, not merely a few."

As he spoke, his ancient eyes leveled on the senator, seeming to mock him. "The girl has refused her biological paternity.

Therefore her formal recognition should be returned to the line of her grandfather. It is my opinion, and I will certainly present it as such to His Eminence the Emperor, that the girl be named Hollin's daughter."

"She is not my grandfather's daughter," George blustered. "She has no father unless our father says she does. Without his recognition, she's a bastard, nothing more, with no claim at all to that legacy."

"Stay out of it, George," Kricket growled. "I'd much rather be named Da's daughter. He was more a father to me anyway. He loved me, wanted me, said I was worth the lot of you combined."

"Is that true?" Coltame asked in an almost giddy tone before he could help himself. He wasn't sure how it happened, but suddenly things had turned around and were proving far too good to be true. Divine intervention again? If she was declared Hollin's daughter, she would be considered Rheigan, despite her blood. She'd be held to Rheigan authority, and Cronus would have no legal claim to her at all. It was brilliant.

"Yeah," Steven replied in an amused tone, nodding his head up and down until his next oldest brother reached out and physically smacked him on the head.

"So witnessed," Coltame nearly purred, "from the senator's acknowledged son."

"I will not stand for this!" Cronus roared, banging his hand loudly down on the table's surface. "The child has been proven to be biologically my offspring. I have acknowledged that she is my offspring. I have submitted proof to the legitimacy of the union between myself and her mother. I have offered formal recognition. She is too young to decide if she will or will not accept my recognition and too ignorant of our customs to understand what she's doing by denying it. By refusing, her actions during this sham of a formal hearing have proven that she is an uncultured, rustic colonial incapable of arguing her case and, quite possibly, not of sound mind. I demand that she be released from this irresponsible union, which the *Nadir*'s own

CHAPTER ELVEN

physicians have testified was not consummated, and placed in my care until such time that she can be properly educated and reintroduced into society."

"I don't want to go with you!" Kricket answered heatedly.

"He's an imperial Rheigan; you are Delsheni royal blood through Meera's daughter and myself. You and your brothers are the great grandchildren of Empress Avala herself. A connection linking you to an ancestry of the most prestigious Delsheni aristocracy - to a line of Delsheni emperors that goes back over ten-thousand years. A union between the two of you is unacceptable, and as soon as Prince Rastmus realizes who and what you are, he will agree with me," he answered, for the very first time addressing her directly. Rastmus's son or not, he would not condone a union between his progeny and the emperor's—not unless they were under his control anyway.

"If given a choice between a Rheigan who has offered me honest protection and the Delsheni who would have tossed me back to Malizore in exchange for my mother..." she began passionately, standing and facing her would-be father. "I chose the Rheigan."

"That is conjecture," Jaget interrupted. He didn't disagree, but no one could prove otherwise. Security recordings confirmed what the girl said, but it was still the senator's word against Professor DeSirpi, and the Professor's honesty was questionable at best.

"You're Delsheni, Kricket," Her second oldest brother said, speaking for the first time, his frustration and displeasure for her clearly evident on his face. "You can't chose a Rheigan husband."

"Ryan... Da was Rheigan," she rebutted in frustration. At least the version of the legend Dr. Xnam had told her about said he was. "Or didn't you know that?"

Absolute silence met her statement as everyone simply stared at her. Hollin had been a Delsheni hero, the origins of his birth rarely mentioned.

"Actually, he was the half-brother of our beloved emperor,"

Goman supplied, eyes twinkling merrily as he broke the silence. "Many considered him the favorite to assume the throne when his father died. Our Emperor Zoujin's tapping came as quite a surprise to a great many people."

Again, silence. Hollin had betrayed the emperor, had been banished, all talk of him forbidden. No one was willing to comment least they face the repercussions it might bring.

"Is the only snag in that contract the fact that the marriage wasn't consummated?" she asked candidly, eyes angrily fixing on the captain. It had to be the dumbest reason she had ever heard, but her so-called father had brought it up more than once, and if that was all there was to it, then she'd do just about anything to keep them from sending her away with him.

"Yes, for the most part," Jaget answered uncomfortably, stunned by her bluntness.

Kricket gave Cronus a measuring look, shoulders back, chin high and rebellious. She didn't know why he would fight so hard to nullify her chances of staying with Coltame any more than she understood why her prospective husband would offer her a one-year contract knowing he was already pledged to someone else. Given the two choices though, she would rather choose the course that would assure her a way out in a year's time over the potential of never getting out from under, or surviving long enough to get out from under, the will of her biological father.

Stepping back and around her chair, she marched determinedly behind the right side of the table until she stood next to her potential husband. He regarded her curiously as she approached, then rose from his chair altogether, unsure what she had in mind. Without warning, she reached up and grabbed the back of his head with both hands, pulling his face down to her hers and summarily locking her lips to his. She counted to three, which was about all the time she had before he began to fall over from the shock of it, nearly pulling her with him, before she released him and directed the full force of her angry glare at the captain.

"Does that settle it?" she asked defiantly, eyes challenging

CHAPTER ELVEN

him to say no.
"I would think that it does," Jaget responded.

CHAPTER TWELVE

Kricket half sat, half flopped on the narrow couch in the living quarters she'd been sent to. Cronus had stormed out, her brothers filing dutifully behind him, but the others had stayed to continue on with other pressing matters that had nothing to do with her. With only a polite, informal nod in her direction, a Nubalah had been given orders to escort her to the room she was in now, and then the doors had summarily closed behind her. She would have been far more put out than she actually was if she hadn't run headlong into her youngest brother, who'd trailed behind the others in an effort to try and see her.

"What possessed you?" Steven had asked without preamble.

"Someone had to end the argument," she'd responded unrepentantly. "I figured it might as well be me."

"Kricket, this isn't home; you just can't do that. Kissing someone in front of other people—it's like taking your clothes off in public and…It's not done. You've embarrassed all of us, dishonored Prince Coltame, and shamed our father's house."

"He's not my father," she'd growled back.

CHAPTER TWELVE

"Well he sure as hell won't be now. Don't you realize what you've done? You've allied yourself with the grandson of the man who exiled Da and exterminated that entire branch of our family. You're on the wrong side, Kricket. Look it up if you don't believe me. Prince Coltame and the house he's loyal to want our whole family dead."

Now, sitting alone, with only her thoughts for company, she wasn't nearly as confident in herself and her actions and wished more than anything that her mother was there. They'd never been as close as they could have been, even after her brothers had left, but there were so many questions that she needed answers to. She wasn't who she thought she was; no one she knew was what she thought they were. Her life was upside down and sideways, and she wished she hadn't been kept in the dark about her family's past.

Steven had asked her to help him; if she wouldn't help their father, then at least help him. They were trying to resurrect their grandfather's Guardian robot, but he didn't have time to explain how they intended to do it. All he'd said was that the real one had been lost and a new one built, but they couldn't figure out how to get it to work. Their grandfather had left detailed notes, but it was in a code that none of them knew. He wanted her to try and translate them—which was exactly what the Professor had said Cronus needed her mother for.

Did that mean they didn't think that they'd get their mother back? Was that why Cronus had fought so hard for her? She didn't know, and her mind ached with all the insecurities, questions, rejections, and fears that haunted it. She tried to grasp at any memory that might give her a clue about the situation that faced her now, but there wasn't one.

Absently, she fingered a large, gold-plated ring that had belonged to her grandfather. Steven had said their grandfather had wanted it to go to her, but her mother had given it to George instead. It wasn't valuable, simply plated with gold, so their oldest brother had refused to wear it. She remembered the ring, remembered her grandfather wearing it, and was more grateful than anyone would ever know to possess something of his as a keepsake. Steven had apparently retrieved it from the floor where it had been tossed, but she doubted he had retrieved it for her. He wanted her to do something for him. There was very little doubt in her mind that the ring had been given to her in an effort to get her to trust him, but she didn't care; she was happy to have it.

She sighed heavily and ran her fingers roughly through her hair, not sure what to do. The only thing she was sure of was her refusal to go with her biological father. He might have been an ally of her grandfather, an ally of her mother, but he was no friend to her, and it didn't take any special powers or dreams or signs to recognize that. She didn't understand how her mother could have had so many children with someone like him—year after year, baby after baby. She shivered involuntarily at the thought, then pushed it from her mind.

Taking out the small metallic chip he'd also given her, she regarded it critically but had very little idea how to retrieve the data off it. It didn't look like the computer disks that she was used to. It was a little, metallic square, barely larger than the short nail of her smallest finger, and encased in a clear plastic sheath that looked remarkably similar to the laboratory slides she'd made in biology class. She understood that simply staring at it wasn't going to give her the information she wanted, but she wasn't sure how ask for something that would enable her to read it without deepening the hole she'd already dug for herself. She needed information she didn't have: to know who to trust, who she could turn to. With a start, she remembered William was also aboard the *Nadir*, but she hadn't seen him since the previous evening, before she'd signed the contract.

Without bothering to hide her scrutiny, her gaze found its way to the Nubalah at the doorway. He was the third she'd encountered to that point, and she found herself comparing his physical characteristics against the others. He wasn't nearly as broad as the others, but she didn't necessarily think that was because he was younger. He was dressed similarly to the other

CHAPTER TWELVE

two, but the tattoos across his neck and arms were an entirely different pattern. His hair was also styled slightly different, but not so much that the difference was obvious at first glance.

Standing, she approached him carefully, but his eyes remained stoically focused in front of him. "I don't suppose you'd know how I can find William DeSirpi, would you?" she asked, not seriously expecting an answer.

When he didn't reply, she moved as if to slip by him and, to her astonishment, he stepped aside and allowed her access to the door. Surprised and caught off guard, she paused, watching him carefully as she slowly touched the lighted panel that she knew would open the door. Somewhat convinced that he wasn't going to stop her, yet still expecting him to, she cautiously stepped through the doorway and was stunned when he simply fell in step behind her.

The outside hallway was not the calm and vacant place that it had been when she entered. It was packed to capacity with a large group of boisterous women surrounding a man who was arguing very loudly with another man about some sort of lodging and why it was unavailable. Finally the second man had the guards push the crowd back down the hall.

"You missed one," he snapped in an agitated voice, indicating Kricket, but when the guard went to shoo her along with the rest of the women, the Nubalah stepped forward and silently, but firmly, prevented him from touching her.

"Well, what are you waiting for?" the man snapped rudely, looking directly at her. "You can't be up here; it's not allowed. I've told the delegate that lodging has been provided in the civilian sector. You can't stay here."

"But I'm not..." Kricket began, pointing to the large group hesitantly, but he simply motioned the guards to push her and her Nubalah down the hall. Not entirely unwilling, she shrugged and allowed herself to be corralled and placed in the large elevator at the end of the hall with the others, then watched as the Nubalah raced to squeeze himself in as the doors closed.

HOLLIN'S HEIR

***

Maerwynn observed as Hollin's daughter sat stoically in her containment cell. Margaret didn't eat, didn't drink, and, if she kept up the hunger strike much longer, she'd soon be dehydrated and in need of medical attention. The solitary cell was devoid of any creature comfort, offering only a hard sleeping platform and crude toilet, but it was better than the original holding pen she'd been tossed into.

She admired the other woman, although she'd never admit it. She had apparently produced five living offspring and had not only lived through it but was still strong enough to passively resist her captors. "Cronus has arrived from Aelis," she said languidly, watching for any reaction from the other woman, but she gave none. "Who would have thought he'd bring four brothers of your troublesome daughter with him."

That got a reaction from her. Margaret's steel gray eyes lifted and leveled on her coldly from behind her dark brown bangs, but she didn't speak, didn't reveal any astonishment.

"That's quite a feat: five living children," Maerwynn continued lazily. "Cronus is touting the natural environment of the planet's colony and a strong bond of love and affection with the mother, but already the news channels are whispering treacherously about laboratory interventions and conspiracies."

She paused, her eyes narrowing on the woman in front of her. She was a half breed, although both sides were about as purebred as you could get. Maerwynn's own ancestry was hardly as wholesome.

"Five grandchildren of Hollin," she mused in a deadly tone. "The youngest of them, a little girl with bravery, so they say, to surpass even her grandsire…five remarkable children…and five components of the legendary Sentinel Guardian just waiting to reappear. Such a truly amazing development, no? What is it the legend says?" she murmured, finger coming up to her lips as if pretending to remember. "Always five, working in unison as

CHAPTER TWELVE

one..."

Margaret's eyes bore coldly into the other woman, but she continued to say nothing. She simply sat there, not resisting, but not complying either.

"In any event," Maerwynn sneered cruelly over her shoulder as she turned and walked slowly down the short cell block. "I think the price on your head just went up."

***

After what seemed a long and rather overly crowded elevator ride, Kricket waited until the last of the rowdy crowd around her filed through the doors and continued down a long hall. She had no idea where she was, but her surroundings didn't look anything like the section of the ship she'd been in before. The large hallway was lined with several different sets of elevator doors, but the colors on the walls were brighter and filled with advertisements. Watching as the other group turned the corner and disappeared, she moved in the opposite direction and was followed at a slight, respectful distance by the Nubalah.

It didn't take long before the hallway of elevators ended, and she stepped out into a wide open area that totally took her breath away. It was as if she had stepped through a portal and into a large, thriving metropolis. At first she panicked, thinking maybe she'd inadvertently boarded some sort of shuttle and been accidentally taken down to the planet's surface, but, although similar, she knew the cityscape in front of her didn't exist on her world and, if it had, Malizore would have destroyed it by now.

The white, marble-like buildings were fifteen or more stories high, with glass crosswalks jutting back and forth between them over what looked to be the main avenue. There were people everywhere, walking to and fro at various speeds, but no motorized vehicles, just a set of what could loosely be described as open trolleys. To her right and down a ways was what looked like a wide open park with green grass, trees, and water fountains. Most astounding of all, up above was a blue sky, complete with moving clouds.

She stood, completely stunned, and wondered how she could possibly still be on board a spaceship. With just a little touch of panic, she wondered if the elevator had been some sort of transporter and if she was now lost on some unknown alien world. It didn't seem possible that there could be a whole city with a blue sky. A cold chill began to creep through her veins as she suddenly realized she was lost, with absolutely no idea how to get back to where she started.

"Why aren't you in school?" a voice asked, and she whirled in its direction to see a young man in uniform. "Don't panic, kiddo," he chuckled. "You're not in trouble. Is this your first time aboard ship?"

"I'm still on the ship?" she asked hopefully, heart thudding in her chest.

"Yes, you're still on the ship," he soothed indulgently, as if he dealt with newcomers on a daily basis and never ceased to be amused by them. "This is the downtown corridor of the civilian sector."

"It's huge," she said incredulously. "There's a sky up there," she added, pointing like an idiot.

"We're a city of nearly three hundred thousand, with our own economy separate from that of the *Nadir* and her function as a military base," he informed her. "It's not a real sky; it's a holographic illusion. But we get our own sunrise, sunset, and nighttime star-scape, just like you'd see under any other dome, in any other major city. Are you lost?"

"A little," she replied sheepishly. She probably looked like some sort of a country bumpkin who'd never seen a city before. But the fact that it was located in a spaceship made it a marvel to behold, and she couldn't stop herself from turning around and gaping. "I think I took the wrong elevator."

"Elevator?" he asked, frowning a little at the odd word. The girl had a Nubalah with her, so he rationalized that she had to belong to some sort of wealthy officer or professional parents. But she was dressed in standard-issue clothing, so it was almost

CHAPTER TWELVE

impossible to tell where she'd originated from. "Where are your parents?" he asked pointedly.

"Parents?" she asked, caught off guard. "I don't have—I mean...no, I don't...I need to find William DeSirpi. He's a tech of some sort...at least I think he is."

"Why don't you come with me," the officer suggested in a slightly placating tone. "I can escort you as far as the general education building. They should have some record on you and your parents and be able to tell you which academic facility you've been assigned to."

"But I'm not in a school. I mean, I already finished..." she protested, realizing that he was assuming she was far younger than she actually was. That was one of the problems with being at least half a foot shorter than everyone else, and, with dismay, she realized that she didn't have any makeup or jewelry on either, which probably didn't help matters.

"I'm not asking, sweetheart," he responded firmly. "Come on. Let's go."

***

"What do you mean she isn't here?" Coltame roared, eyes murderous and every inch his father's son and heir of the Rheigan monarchy.

"I received confirmation that she was escorted by one of the pages to a smaller guest suite one level down," his secretary frantically explained. "But at the time of her arrival, I had already turned my attention to converting the other rooms for Goman's use. His requirements were very specific, and I couldn't meet with her personally. Confusing things was the arrival of the Degauli delegate and his entourage who needed redirection to the civilian section of the ship. I don't know who sent them to this level for lodging; we simply don't have the capacity."

"She was to be escorted back to my quarters, not the guest hall," the prince snarled in a deadly tone, eyes turning almost black in anger. "You did not have the authority to divert her."

She was missing. The thought terrified him as his mind swirled through any number of possibilities, from abduction by Cronus to murder by an agent of Malizore. They'd been separated less than an hour. How she could have simply vanished, on a ship that recorded nearly every movement its occupants made, baffled him. He didn't even know with any certainty if she'd even made it back to the diplomatic corridor. Had she vanished outside of the captain's conference room? There was no way of knowing, because the security recordings outside that chamber had been taken offline for maintenance sometime during the meeting.

"The manifest wasn't specific…just a notation," Coltame's secretary wailed in panic. How his team had managed to lose a consular guest baffled him. He had well over a decade of experience in ambassadorial administration but had only served the young prince for a few months. His current assignment to assist the Rheigan ambassador, and son of the favored choice for succession, was to have been the panicle of his career, but suddenly all his ambitions seemed to come crashing down around him. "The request was tabbed as lodging. She's not registered in the system. I simply assumed…I had no idea, I assigned—"

Turning from his secretary and addressing the head guard directly, Coltame snapped, "Alert security, inform the captain she's missing, and we can't exclude the possibly that she's been abducted again. I want all traffic off this ship stopped. Scan every recording of the hallways she would have taken to get here. If that doesn't yield the information we need, then begin a systematic scan of every security tape, in every hallway, of the entire ship. I want her found," he growled in a deadly tone.

***

"Unfortunately our main computers are still down while the *Nadir* does an unscheduled maintenance," a woman who had

CHAPTER TWELVE

identified herself as some sort of school administrator commented absently as she sat down behind her desk. "But we were finally able to confirm your name and age from your palm scan—even if we can't pull your full file. You are correct, it seems." She said, leveling her gaze to Kricket, "You are not an elementary student."

Kricket tried, with all her might, not to scream in frustration at the woman. It was so hard not to come out with a snide remark about her and her school system in general, but she didn't do it. She simply sat in her chair and offered a thin, slightly stressed smile in return. "No," she managed tightly, "I'm not."

"Well," the other woman responded unrepentantly, "I suppose it was a natural mistake. You are, after all, quite petite." *And*, she added silently to herself, *she's not nearly as physically developed as she should be.*

Kricket gnashed her teeth in response but remained still. She was short—she realized that—but just because she had a bit of a baby face without makeup didn't mean the people in front of her had any right to detain her and not listen to her.

The real problem was that she didn't know how old she was. She could tell them her age in planetary years but not in the complex method of telling time that they used. Planetary years were usually counted using a planet's rotation around a sun, but each planet was a little different. Standard time was a universally accepted method that had nothing to do with a planet's calendar; calculating the difference was mind-boggling.

Kricket's failure to provide anything but her name, and her obvious lack of any formalized education, had the local school officials judging her simply on her size. Despite her protests, any request on her part that she contact William or Coltame or even Dr. Xnam had been received with good amounts of indulgent nodding but totally ignored.

Her tests proved she was ignorant of their curriculum but also exceptionally bright, and, despite her protests to the contrary, she'd been shuffled from room to room in an effort to find her an appropriate peer group in a late elementary classroom. In the end, she'd finally put her foot down and refused to be placed anywhere in their system until she spoke with a supervisor who would listen to her claims that she was not a child.

"The question remains," the administrator continued in an aggrieved tone, "just what to do with you."

"If you would contact William or Coltame..." Kricket began, but didn't get very far.

"Young lady, you might not be an elementary student, but you are not registered military personnel, nor are you in any position to be on a first name basis with the Rheigan ambassador."

"I'm married to him," she returned, exasperated and ready to hit something if someone didn't start listening to her.

In response the administrator slowly closed her eyes in a gesture that seemed to indicate she was also struggling to control her patience. "Miss Holland, I can assure you that whatever game you're playing with us is not only unappreciated, it will eventually land you into quite a bit of trouble if you don't cease immediately."

"I'm not playing a game with you. You people aren't listening. You were wrong about my age. You were wrong to try and assign me to a classroom full of kids, Do you think, just possibly, you're also wrong to assume I'm playing a game with you?"

"The ambassador is not married," the woman returned in a placating tone. "And you, my dear, are not only far too young for him, you seem quite unaware that simple Delsheni colonists cannot aspire to unite with the Rheigan monarchy. Besides, a union of that sort would have been broadcast on the news channels, and it has not."

"Your computers are down," Kricket volleyed dryly.

Unimpressed, the administrator attempted to stare her down, rhythmically tapping her fingers for several long seconds as the silence between them stretched on. The girl had a Nubalah that stuck to her like glue wherever she went, so she was obviously

CHAPTER TWELVE

not the destitute her standard-issue clothing suggested she was. There had to be a family member, somewhere, who could shed a little light on the mystery she presented, but, for the moment, she was stuck with her. Finally, she added, "Until the computer system is back online and we can locate the family members responsible for you, I'm going to place you in remedial classes that will bring you up to speed on the most basic, core education requirements. For the rest of the afternoon though, you will attend structured activities that will allow you to interact with your peer group and catch up with any socialization skills you might be lacking in after a colonial upbringing."

"Great..." Kricket droned sarcastically, managing with a supreme effort to keep her eyes level and not allow them to roll. "I can hardly wait."

***

"I think I know where she is," Gage said as he approached his cousin. He was technically off duty and should have been sound asleep in his bunk by now. But Coltame was in an unusually hot and unreasonable temper, so he'd been brought in to mediate between his cousin and the commanders in charge. He didn't mind; the girl and the developing story around her had captivated him just as much as it had everyone else on the ship.

"Here..." he added, activating a screen on the wall of the crowded room. "This is the security tape of the Degauli delegate and his entourage being escorted off the same floor that Kricket was assigned," he said, keying a sequence that launched the images playing on the flat surface of the wall. "If you look here..." he said, pointing and then catching the eye of the two security officers who had joined them. "That's her," he said pointedly, tapping her image with his finger. "There's the Nubalah assigned to her. She was rounded up with all his other wives, and daughters, and sisters, and cousins, and pushed into the internal transportation system. I checked the manifest, and it looks like it took them to the main civilian transfer site. From there, she'd have been stuck. She's not registered in the *Nadir*'s computer system yet, so she wouldn't have been able to get it to take her anywhere else."

"Where did she go from there?" Coltame asked, relieved beyond measure that they had an answer to the question of her disappearance, but also furious at his staff for causing the disappearance in the first place.

"The only place she could go from there is into the city proper," Gage answered.

"Pull the images from every security camera down there," his cousin ordered gruffly. "Find her and get her back up here."

"That might not be possible for a while," one of the security officers admitted uneasily. At the prince's murderous look, he added hastily, "Two more cryptors were found on the *Nadir* last night. All nonessential computers have been taken offline and placed in quarantine. The civilian sectors are completely isolated and shut down. That's what's taken us so long. All communications are basically dead until the boards are screened, system by system, for more cryptors. The city houses and employs over three hundred thousand civilians, none of whom have computer access or even basic communications right now. It's going to be like finding a needle in a haystack, even if she's down there trying to find us."

"All it's going to take is one agent of Malizore who knows who she is, and she's dead," Coltame responded with lethal venom, eyes boring into the security officers in front of him as his own fears began constricting his chest. "Find her."

CHAPTER TWELVE

ABOUT THE AUTHOR

L.G. Ransom was born in Miami, Florida but grew up living in various countries around the world.

She's a black belt in Tae Kwon Do, a photographer, an artist, a scout leader, a breast cancer survivor, and lives in the suburbs of Washington DC with her husband, two incredible children, and Cavalier King Charles Spaniel.

She has created the cover art for several books, including *Hollins Heir*.

For more information about the Sentinel Dawn series, visit LGRansom.com

Made in the USA
Middletown, DE
17 June 2015